ARThurian LeGends

10 BEST ARTHURIAN LEGENDS EVER!

Margaret Simpson

■SCHOLASTIC

Scholastic Children's Books,
Euston House, 24 Eversholt Street,
London, NW1 1DB, UK
a division of Scholastic Limited
London ~ New York ~ Toronto ~ Sydney ~ Auckland
Mexico City ~ New Delhi ~ Hong Kong

First published in the UK under the title *Top Ten*
by Scholastic Ltd, 1998
This edition published 2009

Text copyright © Margaret Simpson, 1998, 2009
Illustrations copyright © Michael Tickner, 1998, 2009

10 digit ISBN 1 407 10816 2
13 digit ISBN 978 1407 10816 2

Typeset by Falcon Oast Graphic Art Ltd.
Printed and bound by Bookmarque Ltd, Croydon, Surrey

10 9 8 7 6 5 4 3 2 1

The right of Margaret Simpson and Michael Tickner to be identified as the author and
illustrator of this work respectively has been asserted by them in accordance with the
Copyright, Designs & Patents Act, 1988.

CONTENTS

INTRODUCTION

Want to read about spells and magic? Wizards and enchantresses? Love and romance? Knights in shining armour, fighting for their ladies' honour? Tournaments, intrigue, unrequited love? They're all here in Arthurian legend, as the Knights of King Arthur's Round Table find themselves faced with tests of courage and honour.

Read about the powerful, all-knowing Merlin; about Arthur's arch-enemy Morgan le Fay; about the Lady of the Lake who lives beneath mysterious waters in the land of Avalon; about the glamour of life at the court of Camelot. Go with the knights through forest and over mountain in search of adventure. Read about a knight who can put his head back on after it has been cut off; about a Bleeding Spear which hangs in the air dripping with blood...

Was there a real King Arthur? No one really knows, but if there was, he would have lived at the very end of the 5th century AD – when the Roman Empire fell apart. As soon as the Romans were off the scene the Saxons started to invade Britain. We don't know much about those centuries because no one wrote anything down much. That's why we call them the "Dark Ages", because they are shrouded in mystery. The stories we know today were written down between the 12th and 15th centuries (the Middle Ages). That's why they are full of knights in armour and damsels in distress.

There are literally hundreds of stories about King Arthur and his knights and it's hard choosing ten stories out of so many – but here they are – the Ten Best Stories of Arthurian Legend ... Ever!

LEGEND 1: THE SWORD IN THE STONE

After Uther Pendragon (Pendragon means "Chief Soldier") died, the land of Britain had no king. All the lords and chieftains fought each other, each wanting the crown for himself. They robbed farmers and shopkeepers, and forced people to fight for them. Everyone was getting sick of it, and longing for a good, strong ruler who would keep the robber barons in order.

One day that ruler appeared – but he wasn't what people expected. If there had been tabloid newspapers in those days, this is how they might have reported the first of the Ten Best legends about King Arthur.

Celtic Clarion

Winter Solstice Edition

Stone Me! Where Did It Come From?

Worshippers attending the service on Christmas morning in London's biggest Abbey were

"STONE ME!" LIONEL LOOKS ON IN WONDER.

astonished to see a huge slab of marble appear from nowhere in the churchyard.

"One minute there was just a grassy mound beyond the tombstones," said Lionel Fazakerly, a squire aged 14. "Next time I looked there was this ginormous marble slab with a sword sticking out the top. It just seemed to have materialised out of thin air."

Lionel was one of the hundreds of knights and squires unable to find room in the crowded church on Christmas morning. He and his friends, eager to join in the service, gathered in the churchyard, despite the biting cold wind.

"It definitely didn't drop from the sky. There was no thud," said Lionel. When asked if he thought it might have been pushed or wheeled into place, he said, "Impossible. There is no way a stone that size could have been manoeuvred without a lot of noise."

The minute the stone appeared, witnesses rushed into the church to tell the Archbishop of Canterbury what had happened. But the Archbishop insisted on finishing his sermon and said no one was to move till High Mass was over.

"True-born King of Britain" written in stone

After the service, the Archbishop and leading knights went to examine the stone. On it they found the following message carved in gold:

> " WHOEVER PULLS THIS SWORD FROM THIS STONE IS THE TRUE BORN KING OF ALL BRITAIN."

Immediately every knight there jostled and pushed his way forward to try his luck. Some tried to wrench it out, others tried to ease it gently as if it were a key. But although the highest in the land were at the service that morning, not one of them could shift the sword.

As knight after knight failed, the Archbishop spoke. "It is obvious the man born to be king is not here today," he said. "On New Year's Day we will hold a special tournament, and each knight can try again." He ordered messengers to ride the length and breadth of the land to announce this.

At the Archbishop's command, ten knights were left guarding the stone.

KNIGHT AFTER KNIGHT AND STILL NO JOY!

Is it Merlin's magic?

As the failed knights melted away in the darkening winter's afternoon, rumours started to spread among the common people. Mistress Jane Alwynne, a 45-year-old grandmother from Westminster, was just one of the people sure that the stone had something to do with the mysterious wizard, Merlin. "He is the only one who could magic up something like this," she said.

Merlin, a mysterious old man who lives as a recluse in the valleys of North Wales, was seen in London last week. Sources close to the Archbishop say that the two have been holding secret talks.

WHAT DID THE WIZARD SAY TO THE BISHOP?!

If this is true, the *Clarion* wants to know: Is the Archbishop in league with Merlin? If so, why? What can a Christian priest have to say to a man who dabbles in magic?

Celtic Clarion

2 January

God save the King!
Sword drawn from stone by 15-year-old boy

Yesterday the mysterious sword was finally pulled from the stone outside Westminster Abbey – by a boy not yet old enough to be a knight! Today we can reveal the lad's identity. His name is Arthur, and he is the fifteen-year-old son of Sir Ector, Knight of the Realm.

"THIS'LL DO!" THINKS 'HAVE-A-GO' ARTHUR!

At first Sir Kay, 21, ambitious elder son of Sir Ector, claimed he was the one who dislodged the sword. Kay, recently knighted, had arrived with young Arthur to fight in the tournament – but at the last moment discovered he had forgotten his sword. He sent his younger brother Arthur back to his lodgings to fetch it. On his way, Arthur saw the churchyard was deserted. All ten knights who had been guarding the stone had gone to the tournament. He decided to take the sword in the stone. "I thought it would be quicker," he told his father later.

Kay claims credit

Kay recognized the sword as soon as he saw it. He knew what it meant – and he wasn't going to let his younger brother rule the kingdom. The slimy rascal ran to his father, and told him that he had pulled it from the stone – so he was King of Britain! Luckily for Arthur, Ector had seen Kay fail the day before. He took him to the Abbey, and made Kay swear on the Bible what had really happened. Reluctantly, Kay admitted that it was Arthur who had brought him the sword.

Still suspicious, Sir Ector questioned the younger boy.

"Did you really pull it from the stone?" he demanded. Not satisfied when Arthur said yes, he put the sword back in the marble slab and demanded Arthur draw it again for him to see.

Knife in butter

But first Kay and his father decided to have another go – only to find that the sword was stuck fast once more. Finally, they stepped aside – and the boy Arthur, not yet knighted, slid the sword from the stone. "To him it was as easy as pulling a knife out of a pat of butter," said an onlooker.

So a young boy is the new King of Britain. But not everyone is happy about this. Many have refused to serve under a boy his age; others say that the sword in the stone was a trick.

To these doubters, the *Clarion* says: SOUR GRAPES! They would not be doubting if their son had pulled the sword from the stone. This country has been without a king too long.

So the *Clarion* says: Well done, sir! God Save King Arthur!

"'TWAS NOTHING!" SAYS THE YOUNG BLADE!

Celtic Clarion

3 January

Shock horror! "Arthur not my son," says Sir Ector

The *Clarion* can reveal exclusively that Arthur, King of Britain, is not all he seems. In an interview given to this paper Sir Ector said, "I have no idea who Arthur's real parents are. All I know is that Merlin brought a baby boy to me, fifteen years ago, and asked me to rear him as my own. This I did, and that boy is Arthur."

SIR ECTOR,........LEFT HOLDING THE BABY!

Already there are many knights who refuse to kneel to Arthur. The *Clarion* has stood firm against them.

But this news damages the boy's claim. If he is not Ector's son, who is he?

WHO ART ARTHUR?

The *Clarion* demands that if Merlin knows the truth, he should come clean NOW.

COME ON MERLIN, "SPELL" IT OUT!!!!

15

Celtic Clarion

Easter

War looms
Right royal rebellion – Six kings march on Arthur

Civil war seemed inevitable last night as six kings from the wild fringes of Britain told King Arthur to expect a visit. The Kings of Orkney and Lothian, Gwynydd and Powys, Gorre and Garloth announced they were coming to Camelot with "presents" for the young king.

calling himself King of all Britain," said the King of Lothian. He would not say what the "presents" were that he was carrying, but one of his men laughed, jabbed his sword and said, "We're going to make sure Arthur gets the point." "Arthur won't even be King of Westminster by this time

RATTLED ROYALS RANT AND RAVE !

"We are fed up with this slip of a boy who has jumped up from nowhere

next week," added this man, who refused to be named.

Celtic Clarion

Crisis Edition

King flees

In a desperate attempt to shake off his enemies, the young King Arthur has fled with Merlin and many of his knights to Caerleon Castle in South Wales. The six kings went after him and now have the castle surrounded and under siege.

DIRTY RASCALS SURROUND KING OF THE CASTLE!!

"It's just a matter of time," said the King of Lothian. "We will soon starve him out."

Local people say it may take longer than he thinks. For some weeks now they have seen supplies of food going into the castle.

RIGHT ROYAL RATIONS!

Military experts say that the castle of Caerleon is impossible to attack. If it is well-stocked with food, the six kings may have to wait a long time.

The *Clarion* says: Go home to your boggy kingdoms, Bumpkins! It'll take more than a few wild men from the hills to conquer a British King!

17

Celtic Clarion

Exclusive! The full story!
Merlin comes clean
Magic and royal blood in Arthur's past

Arthur is the son of Uther Pendragon, and he spent his baby years in the magic land of Avalon, where fairies and elves blessed him with the gifts of virtue and strength.

So said Merlin, in an amazing, hour-long speech from the battlements, fifteen days after the siege of Caerleon began. He told his listeners, friend and foe, that it was hopeless to wage war on Arthur.

"He was born to be King over all of you," he boomed. "You remember Uther Pendragon, who led you to victory over the Saxons?"

Loud cries of "Aye," and "Yea, God rest him," rose from the knights on both sides of the castle wall.

"Arthur is the son of Uther and Igrayne," boomed Merlin.

This news was met by scandalized silence. Then people began to mutter. As everyone knows, sixteen years ago Igrayne was the wife of Duke Gorlois.

"Uther came to me and told me of his love," Merlin went on. "I made an agreement with him.

UTHER LOVES IGRAYNE! TRUE!!

I told him I would cast a spell on him so that when he came to Igrayne she would see the form of her husband Gorlois. In return—" and here the old magician paused to make sure that everyone was listening. "In return he would give to me the child they would make. Uther agreed. He visited Igrayne at Tintagel, and she saw not Uther her king, but Gorlois her husband. Even though—" and the old man smiled his mysterious smile. "Even though at that very moment Gorlois lay dead of a battle wound."

Merlin admits: "I took infant Arthur"

"A child was born as a result of that night," Merlin went on, "and true to his word, Uther gave that child to me.

MERLIN'S PRIZE FOR HELP IN PASSION PLOT!

"I carried the infant away one stormy night, down the steep cliff path to the sea. Uther married Igrayne, but they had no more children. In the few years left to him, Uther brought up the three daughters of Gorlois as his own. Lot, King of Orkney," Merlin shouted down to the knights below the battlement, "your wife Morgause, is one of them. Nantres, King of Garlot, your wife Elaine another, and Morgan le Fay was the third daughter of Gorlois. Of her, let no more be said," the old man said with a shiver.

MORGAN GIVES MERLIN THE HEEBIE-JEEBIES!!

Avalon calling! Three fairy gifts

The people listened in silence as Merlin continued his fantastic tale. "Uther's own child, the royal child, spent his baby years in Avalon. My country, the land of magic! The beings who live there – who you in your ignorance call fairies,

BABY ARTHUR IS AWAY WITH THE FAIRIES !!!

elves, imps – cast a spell upon the child.

"They gave him three gifts: to be the best of all knights, to be the greatest king this land shall ever have, and to live longer than any other man. At this very moment, in Avalon, those same fairies are forging a special sword for Arthur, one that can only ever be raised for a good cause. That sword they will send to us when the time is right. And when the time is right, they will call that same sword back again to Avalon."

"Britain is God's kingdom on Earth," Merlin warns Northern Kings

Merlin finished his long speech by addressing the Northern Kings directly. "Make no mistake, Lot, King of Orkney!" he shouted. "Nantres, King of Garlot, do you hear? Arthur is your king, too. For his kingdom is not simply the land of Britain. Arthur's kingdom is more than Britain. It is Logres, land of blessing! It is God's kingdom upon Earth, which Arthur has been sent to show you for a short while until the darkness falls again."

MERLIN TALKS THEM ROUND!

ARTHUR STEPS OUT !

After this astonishing claim, knights inside and outside the castle knelt in homage as Arthur appeared above Merlin on the steps. Then all the knights, including those who fought against Arthur, swore they would serve him as true and faithful subjects. Once again, it became clear how important Merlin is to the people. Thanks to him, the civil war is over.

At a signal from Merlin, the Archbishop of Canterbury appeared and set the crown on Arthur's head.

"This marks the true beginning of Arthur's reign," said Merlin. Then Arthur himself spoke, and a great cheer went up at his message.

"Today we have stopped fighting amongst ourselves," he said. "Tomorrow the real fight begins. Tomorrow we will drive the Saxons out of Britain!"

The *Clarion* **says: AMEN to that!**

21

FANTASTIC FACTS 1: WHO'S WHO, WHERE'S WHERE AND WHAT'S WHAT IN ARTHURIAN LEGEND

THE OTHERWORLD

1 Merlin: Weird old man, part-priest, part-magician. He always knows what's happening, mainly because he's usually pulling the strings. He is friends with the Christian Archbishop, although he belongs to the old Celtic pagan religion – in fact he was a Druid priest or high priest, and every bit as important as the Archbishop – though the bish' probably didn't think so.

2 The Lady of the Lake: A supporter of Merlin and part of his mysterious set-up. Sometimes only one of her arms makes an appearance, always dressed in white samite (silk to you). At other times she walks on water, or even appears at court.

There is some confusion

about her name – some of the stories say she is called Morgan, some Nimuë. This is probably because she is part of the Avalon set-up, where according to the *Life of Merlin*, "Nine sisters rule". So we're lucky the medieval storytellers didn't give her nine different names! ·

3 Avalon: A country way off the beaten track, beyond forest and mountain, inhabited by magical beings with powers to help ordinary mortals.

First mentioned in a very old text called the *Life of Merlin*, which calls it, "the island of apples which men call the fortunate isle ... the fields there have no need of farmers. Of its own accord it produces grain and grapes and apple trees." A sort of paradise, in fact.

4 Morgan le Fay: The first stories portray her as beautiful and good – one of the nine sisters who rule Avalon. "She who is first of them is more skilled in the healing art and excels her sisters in the beauty of her person," says the *Life of Merlin*. "Morgan is her name and she can cure sick bodies... She can change her shape, fly, go where she likes." However, by medieval times, Morgan had become an out-and-out

baddie. She did not lose her magical powers – she just used them in evil plots to try and destroy King Arthur. She is usually described as the youngest of Arthur's three half-sisters, and not very pleased about it. The good gal from Avalon is now:

5 Nimuë: Sometimes called the Lady of the Lake, she helps King Arthur and rescues him from Morgan's evil plots. Merlin fancies her like mad. He turns himself into a handsome squire to woo her, and teaches her his magic spells. She wants the spells, but she doesn't fancy Merlin.

THE COURT

6 King Arthur: In Arthurian legend he is a medieval king, strong and chivalrous, uniting his country and driving out the Saxon invaders, and making all his knights live up to very high standards. King Arthur may have fought the Saxons, but he would not have been a knight in shining armour. He was a a Celtic chieftain, in all  likelihood a head-hunter, painting himself with woad and wearing his hair in a Mohican!

7 Queen Guinevere: The daughter of King Leodegrance (Lee-o-der-grance), said in the earliest legends to be beautiful and brave. Merlin warned Arthur against marrying her, but Arthur wouldn't listen. The medieval storytellers had a bit of a problem with her, because by their time the Christian Church was very powerful, and the Church thought it was better to be good than be brave. In the eyes of the Church, Guinevere was not good – she spent her whole married life in love with Sir Lancelot. However, the storytellers went ahead and

called her virtuous (a posh word for good) anyway – at least till the end of Arthur's reign.

8 Sir Lancelot du Lac: In medieval legend he was King Arthur's best friend – even though he was in love with Arthur's wife! Considered to be the bravest of all the Knights of the Round Table, he was called "*du Lac*" (which is French for "of the Lake") because he was kidnapped by the Lady of the Lake. What happened was, when he was a baby, the castle where he was living (in North Berwick, near Edinburgh) was set on fire. His mum and dad – Queen Helen and King Ban – had just managed to get him out alive when his dad had a heart attack. His mum put him down at the roadside while she tried to help her husband, and what do you know, along came the Lady of the Lake (dressed in white  samite) and whisked him away to her underwater palace.

In courtly language Lancelot is the Queen's "champion" which means he wears her favours (a scarf) in battle, and he isn't free to champion other ladies. He never marries and whenever he fancies another woman, Guinevere gives him a hard time.

9 The Round Table: A wedding present from King Leodegrance, Guinevere's father, to his son-in-law, which Arthur's father, Uther Pendragon had given to him. One hundred and fifty knights could sit round it at one time, so it must have been huge. Each knight was

given his own special seat, and some seats remained empty until their owners came to claim them. For example, one seat, immediately to the right of the King known as the Siege Perilous ("siège" is French for seat or chair) remained empty. When he was asked why, Merlin said, "Only one man can sit there, and he will be the best man in the world. If anyone else tries to take his place, he shall die immediately!" The man who was able to sit in it safely did not show up for twenty years!

10 Camelot: The place where Arthur held his court. Legend says it was built by Merlin in a single night. No one knows exactly where it was but most parts of the British Isles make a claim to Camelot. Winchester Castle and Cadbury Castle, both in southern England,

Caerleon in Wales, and Stirling Castle in Scotland have all been put forward as the "real" Camelot.

LEGEND 2: EXCALIBUR!

Arthurian legends are full of stories about fate and destiny: writing appears by magic on seats, saying who should sit on them; a sword appears which can only be drawn by one particular person. Arthur proved he was king by pulling the sword from the stone, but there is an even more famous sword with which he is connected. Here is story number two:

ARTHUR GETS THE POINT

THE STORY SO FAR.....
ONE DAY, KING ARTHUR WAS OUT RIDING ON HIS OWN WHEN HE SAW MERLIN IN TROUBLE.....

HE'LL PULL THROUGH.

OF COURSE, I KNOW.

MERLIN WAS RIGHT. IN THREE DAYS, THE YOUNG KING HAD RECOVERED COMPLETELY FROM HIS WOUNDS.

I FEEL NAKED WITHOUT MY SWORD.

DON'T WORRY, I'VE GOT A NEW ONE LINED UP FOR YOU.

WHERE IS IT?

YOU'LL SEE

THE FURTHER THEY RODE, THE WILDER AND MORE DESOLATE WAS THE COUNTRYSIDE.

BENEATH THIS LAKE IS A HUGE ROCK. IN THE ROCK IS A FANTASTIC PALACE, AND IN THE PALACE IS A LADY. ASK HER NICELY AND SHE MIGHT GIVE YOU YOUR SWORD.

I AM THE LADY OF THE LAKE. YOUR SWORD, EXCALIBUR IS READY. ALL YOU HAVE TO DO TO GET IT IS SWEAR THAT WHEN I ASK A FAVOUR FROM YOU, IT WILL BE GRANTED.

ANYTHING YOU LIKE, I SWEAR ON MY HONOUR AS A KNIGHT.

THEN CLIMB ABOARD.

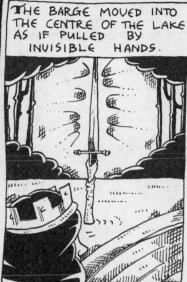

THE BARGE MOVED INTO THE CENTRE OF THE LAKE AS IF PULLED BY INVISIBLE HANDS.

AS ARTHUR TOOK THE SWORD EXCALIBUR, THE ARM DISAPPEARED BENEATH THE SURFACE OF THE LAKE.

HERE COMES THAT BEGGAR PELLINORE AGAIN. I BET I CAN SORT HIM OUT WITH EXCALIBUR.

LET HIM PASS.

FANTASTIC FACTS 2: EVERYTHING YOU EVER WANTED TO KNOW ABOUT MERLIN THE MAGICIAN AND A FEW THINGS YOU DIDN'T...

Merlin. Funny name. I thought a Merlin was a bird. You're absolutely right. It's a kind of falcon. But Merlin wasn't called Merlin originally.

What was he called then? Myrrdin. It's Welsh and it means "sea fortress". Britain was known as Clas Myrrdin (Merlin's enclosure) before anyone lived in it.

Why did he change his name to Merlin? He didn't. It was changed by the French storytellers of the Middle Ages.

Why? Because Myrrdin sounds a bit like "merde" which is French for poo!

Charming! Especially when you're Chief Druid.

Merlin was Chief Druid? You mean he was one of those guys who get dressed up in white and try to make their way to Stonehenge on Midsummer night?

Among other things. In Arthur's time, Druids played a more important role.

For instance?

Well, according to Julius Caesar: "The Druids officiate at the worship of the gods, regulate public and private sacrifices and give rulings on all religious questions..."

So they were busy bods.

Yes, but on the other hand, according to Caesar, they were excused from military service, and they didn't have to pay tax.

Do we know how Merlin got to be Chief Druid?

Yes. But you'd better get comfortable, it's a long story.

Go on.

He came to the fore when a fierce ruler called Vortigern was trying to build a wall around a castle. The wall kept falling down, and Vortigern sent for all the Welsh wizards, or Druids, to tell him why. One of them called Joram said that if they found a boy with no father, and mixed his heart's blood with the lime of the wall, then the wall would stand till the end of time. Merlin was this boy. When his mother was fifteen she started to have visions of a knight in gold armour. Then the knight in gold disappeared and was never seen again. Merlin was born soon afterwards.

A likely tale.

Look, do you want me to tell you, or don't you?

Yes, yes.

Then no more clever comments.

Vortigern's soldiers heard other boys taunting Merlin and saying he had no father. (Merlin was ten years old.) When they brought him to the wall, Merlin realized that Joram had set him up, and he would die. So he told Vortigern that Joram was talking nonsense, and that he knew why the wall kept falling down. Merlin proposed a deal whereby if he told Vortigern the reason, and was proved right, Joram would be put to death. Merlin said there was water beneath the castle's foundations, and when Vortigern's men dug a ditch, they found he was right. Not only that. Merlin went on to tell everybody, "There are two dragons living in the water. One is milk-white  and the other blood-red. Every night they fight, and the upheaval makes the wall fall down." Then Merlin gave orders for the water to be drained.

As the water drained away, sure enough, two dragons reared up from the silt at the bottom. The King had Joram's head cut off, and from that time onwards, Merlin became the King's adviser.

Wow! How did Merlin know about the dragons?

I think we can assume that right from the start he had special powers.

You mean he knew all this without being taught?

No. He had a teacher, whose name was Bleys. When last seen, Bleys was living in a cave on the island of Orkney. One day, when the lords were still quarrelling about whether they would accept Arthur as King, Bleys sent for Morgause, Queen of Orkney. Morgause found him so shrunken with age that he looked like a monkey. He told her that he and Merlin had been with Uther Pendragon the night he died, leaving no son behind. After he died, the two magicians left the castle and went down to the beach. Suddenly a light appeared, and they could make out a ship shaped like a dragon. Aboard it they could see groups of shining beings.

It disappeared as suddenly as it had come. The magicians stood on the shore as black wave after black wave broke on the dark sand. Then, on the ninth wave, a naked child rode into shore. Merlin picked him up, crying, "The King! Here is Uther's heir!"

The child was Arthur, said Bleys. There should be no more quarrelling. Having told Morgause this story, Bleys drew his last breath and died. But when Morgause asked Merlin about it, he wasn't letting on.

Crafty beggar. Anything else he's famous for?
Yes. Just the little matter of Stonehenge. One story says that Merlin had it shipped over stone by stone from Ireland. And there was no Parcel Force in those days, remember.

Not to be confused with: Mel Gibson, Meryl Streep, a grey and blue merlin falcon, or any old party conjuror.

Least likely to say: Don't ask me, I'm only human.

Most likely to say: Keep your eye on that scabbard, Art, if you know what's good for you.

LEGEND 3: KING ARTHUR AND QUEEN GUINEVERE

Arthur spent the first ten years of his reign seeing off the Saxon invaders and subduing rebel barons. When at last peace reigned in the Kingdom of Logres, Merlin told him it was time he looked for a wife, and asked if he had anyone in mind. Arthur said he was in love with a young woman he had met the previous year – Guinevere, daughter of King Leodegrance of Cameliarde (camel-e-ard). Merlin, who could see into the future, warned him this was not a wise choice. "She is very beautiful," he told Arthur, "but it will all end in tears. Your best knight will fall in love with her and there will be civil war over her."

Arthur did not listen. Instead he sent to King Leodegrance, asking for Guinevere's hand in marriage. King Leodegrance was very pleased. Soon Guinevere – and the Round Table – were on their way to Camelot, escorted by Arthur's trusted friend, Sir Lancelot du Lac. The date for the wedding was set for the Feast of Pentecost.

A month earlier, *C17*, the top-selling Celtic mag for trendy teens, published the following feature, in which an unknown princess asked for advice:

STAND BY YOUR MAN

Who says it's all fun being a Celtic princess? I come from a royal family, and a while ago another royal came to visit the olds. He wasn't bad looking, and I could see he liked me. Two months ago this guy sent word to the 'rents asking

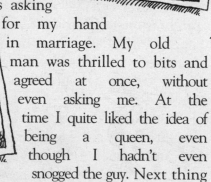

for my hand in marriage. My old man was thrilled to bits and agreed at once, without even asking me. At the time I quite liked the idea of being a queen, even though I hadn't even snogged the guy. Next thing

I knew I was on my way to his palace, escorted by his best mate. It was a long journey which took weeks because we had to cart this huge round table my old man insisted on sending as my dowry. Well – you probably guessed it – I fell in love with his mate. Lance is tall, dark and handsome, with these sexy scars on his face. He has great legs, he's strong but gentle and chivalrous at the same time. I hoped that when I met the hunky royal again, the sight of him would drive all thoughts of Lance from my mind…

It hasn't worked. My husband-to-be is a good bloke, but I can't get his best mate out of my mind. Those days on the road with him were the happiest of my life. At night the servants pitched our tents in a sheltered valley or woodland glade, and together with our ladies- and gentlemen-in-waiting we ate a supper cooked on the campfire, and listened to the latest songs played on the lute late into the night. He kept saying stuff about my hair and clothes and how great I looked. I know you will say this was just knightly courtesy, but you didn't see the way he looked at me.

What am I to do? There'll be a scandal. My husband will be hurt and the 'rents will disown me if I pull out of the marriage now. I long to be alone with Lance and ask him if he feels the same, but since our arrival at Court he seems to be avoiding me. In one week's time the door will close for ever. I can't stand thinking of Lance in someone else's arms. Should I speak out before it is too late?

G. de L., Camelot

We asked three well-known columnists what advice they would give to G. de L. This is what they said:

DO YOUR DUTY, GIRL, AND FORGET HIM

Dear G. de L.,
What a spoilt, silly damsel you are. Do you really think a few evenings camping beneath the stars are a sound basis on which to build a good marriage?

Your father obviously has your interests at heart. He has found you a good husband who will give you a fabulous position in society, but you, it seems, won't be happy until you have brought disgrace on both your family and your husband.

All knights are capable of making a lady feel special, it's part of their training. If what you say is true, and this man has been making overtures to you on his own behalf while pretending to speak for his lord, then he is not worthy of the rank of knighthood.  If, as I think, you have allowed a little moonlight, and a fine pair of legs to go to your head, then by speaking out you will embarrass the knight, and also throw away any chance of happiness with your husband.

The fact that Lance is avoiding you speaks volumes. It means that either he knows he overstepped the mark, or that you are reading more into his words and looks than he meant. Either way, you should forget him, and look to your husband. Over time it will become easier, and you will have the comfort of knowing that you have **done the right thing**!

WHO'S BOSS HERE?

Dear G. de L.,

The fact that you were bringing with you a round table of considerable size suggests that you are the sovereign of a large kingdom – *in your own right.* I wonder therefore that you say this match was

arranged for you by your father without your consent. Where was your mother in all this, for it was from her that you inherited your position? It sounds as if your family has forgotten our great Celtic tradition – that it is up to the Queen

to choose her mate from among the strongest and bravest warriors.

What you have to think about here are not your personal feelings, but the kingdom. Who will make the better king? Forget the rubbish taught by the

Church – you do not have to stay married to this man till death do you part. If, as the years go by, you find him a poor king or poor husband – take a new mate! But you do need to sort out the ground-rules, like who is

boss, and who is doing the choosing.

Remember, there are powerful forces at work

trying to end our Celtic ways, and reduce women like yourself to weak, simpering creatures with nothing in their heads but romantic love.

You have a great life ahead of you, provided you are strong and assert yourself. Stop asking other people what to do and *tell* your subjects – and whichever man you choose – **who is boss!**

HAVE THE BEST OF BOTH WORLDS...

Dear G.,

Lighten up! You can marry your king and still enjoy the love of your gorgeous battle-scarred hunk. Haven't you heard of courtly love? It's all the rage in France, but then we French have always been more sophisticated about such things. How it works is that each knight declares his love for the lady he fancies. If you accept him, then all you have to give him is the odd scarf, ring, or if you really want to, a kiss now and again. Then he's yours

for ever, wearing your favours in battle, and defending your honour if anyone dares insult you. It's great fun, and quite different from marriage, which is all about property and inheritance.

What you think of as a terrible dilemma is actually a wonderful stroke of luck. Many damsels would give their eye-teeth to marry a king and also have his right-hand man as their knight! **So make the most of it. Enjoy!**

Here are the names of the three letter-writers who replied to Guinevere. Can you tell who wrote which letter?

a) Top troubadour and bad-boy heart-throb Chrétien de Troyes
b) Hilda, Abbess of York
c) Morgause, Queen of Orkney

FANTASTIC FACTS 3: LOVE IN THE ARTHURIAN LEGENDS

DO ME A FAVOUR

The love affair between Lancelot and Guinevere lasted for nearly thirty years – most of their lives, in fact. At first they played by the rules of courtly love, but as time went on, passion got the better of them. Their affair became a scandal and Sir Lancelot had to flee the country. Then, when King Arthur was away fighting Lancelot in France, Guinevere ran off with – or was kidnapped by – another, younger knight called Mordred. In the war that followed, King Arthur was to die in battle.

All Guinevere's love affairs make poor old Arthur look a bit of an idiot. Didn't he know what was going on? Why didn't he get rid of his wife?

Basically this story is a fascinating example of what happens when the same events are retold by people living at different historical times. The story of Arthur, Guinevere and Lancelot was told over and over again, by different types of people all trying to make it fit in with their beliefs. So what has come down to us has three layers to it.

THE CELTIC:

The real Arthur and Guinevere lived in Celtic Britain. In Celtic times, inheritance passed down the female side.

In other words, in order to become king, you had to marry the queen. In fact, it's possible that "Guinevere" is not a name but a title – a bit like the "Prince of Wales" is today. If that's true, then it means it was marriage to Guinevere which gave Arthur the right to be king.

The trouble with this system, from Arthur's point of view, was that sooner or later the queen could choose another boyfriend, and then that man – usually younger and stronger – would be king. Perhaps Arthur used the old system to get to the top, and then refused to move over for a younger man – this may be one reason why Morgan le Fay hated him so much.

Incidentally, the original story probably didn't include Lancelot at all, because he was invented by a French troubadour – but it did feature other would-be lovers. (Psst – Guinevere –

they're only after your queendom.)

THE CHRISTIAN:

By medieval times the quaint old Celtic marriage customs had died out, and the Christian Church was pushing the idea of marriage to one person for life. Land and titles were now inherited not from mum but from dad, and women were supposed to be pure and good, not powerful and go-getting. But marriages among the nobility were still about land and money, so you might end up marrying some rich old bore you didn't fancy. It was probably because of this that another new idea – courtly love – caught on in such a big way.

THE COURTLY:

Courtly love was definitely not about land and property – it was about **true love**! It started around 1160 among the troubadours. These were originally French minstrels

who wandered from one isolated castle to another, singing songs, reciting poetry, and telling stories. In these stories, every knight chose a lady to defend – and she could be anybody except for his own wife! There weren't any naughty goings-on in the stories, they were more about sighing and longing. They caught on in a big way, especially with powerful 12th century French queens like Eleanor of Aquitaine and Marie de Rais. Just like readers of magazine fiction today, the queens and the ladies of the court wanted to hear about men who treated women chivalrously, were faithful to them, and who protected them.

Churchmen didn't like the ideas of the troubadours at all. They saw them as a threat to morality and marriage.

NB In courtly love, a knight was supposed to

"defend his lady's honour". If someone said she was a two-timing cheat, her champion would fight the man who said it. Her reputation depended on who won the fight!

Late in King Arthur's reign, Queen Guinevere was accused of murdering one of the Knights of the Round Table with a poisoned apple. No one would fight to prove she hadn't done it – so she was going to be burned at the stake. Finally Sir Lancelot heard about it and came riding to her rescue. He won the fight (surprise, surprise) so Guinevere was "not guilty".

LEGEND 4: SIR GAWAIN AND THE GREEN KNIGHT

The knights of King Arthur's court were very keen on adventures. Usually this meant riding off into the countryside and taking a swipe at any law-breakers or troublemakers. One Christmas, however, the challenge came to Camelot itself. Number four of the Ten Best Arthurian Legends Ever, is the story of Gawain and the Green Knight – told by Sir Gawain de Mole in his very own words.

OFF WITH HIS HEAD!

If found please return this diary to:
Sir Gawain de Mole d'Orkney, aged 22$\frac{1}{2}$
Camelot
Logres
Albion
Europe
The World
The Universe

Christmas Eve
Arrived at court this afternoon. Traffic very

bad, every knight and squire in the kingdom seemed to be heading for Camelot. The roads were really churned up by all the horses' hooves.

I wonder who'll be chosen to tell the court about his best adventure this past year. I bet it will be old Lancelot, he gets picked every time.

Still, at least he has decent adventures, which is more than can be said for some of the others. Haven't had too good a year for adventures myself, what with the unfortunate accident when the lady wife of Blamoure ran into my sword when I was finishing off her husband. I was very lucky there wasn't a Public Enquiry.

Am planning to wear my new tabard and leggings for the feast tomorrow, in the hope that Eleanor may notice me at last. Gaheris says that he saw her talking on the battlements with Sir Lancelot. He said they were standing very close, but I don't believe him. Everyone knows Sir Lancelot is the Queen's Knight, so how can he be interested in Eleanor?

I wish Eleanor would notice me. Perhaps if I

do something really heroic in the next twelve months, I'll get her attention.

January 1st

What a start to the year! I'm still stunned with shock and it's all Eleanor's fault. If she hadn't ignored me I wouldn't have needed to try and impress her.

The day began all right. We all went to church as usual, the whole court, then we came back and stuffed ourselves to the gills with roast boar, and venison, and goose and partridge. Then, after the King's Speech, we were just settling down for a snooze-making recital of Lancelot's adventures (I said it would be Lancelot again), when there was the most terrible clatter of hooves outside. It sounded as if there was an army arriving! Then the doors of the hall were flung open, and into the hall rode the most ginormous knight on the most ginormous horse. At first I thought I'd drunk too much mead, because it seemed to me the knight was green. I don't mean just his clothes, I mean his hair, his skin – everything.

In one hand he had a bough of holly, and in the other a huge green axe. Then he threw down the holly branch and yelled out in this terrifying voice:

"So who's the boss round here?"

No one spoke. We were all scared stiff. Then Uncle Arthur spoke up.

"Welcome, Sir Knight. Why don't you take a seat and join the feast?" he said. Which was a pretty cool way to talk to a green giant, I thought. It's times like this that you know why Uncle Arthur's king.

"That's not what I'm here for," said the knight. "But don't worry, I'm not here to make war. Otherwise I wouldn't have left my armour at home. I come from the north, where I've heard stories about the bravery and virtue of the Knights of the Round Table. So I thought I'd liven up your Yule festivities. Here's the deal. If any man in this hall is brave enough, I will give him this axe..." At this he held the huge green axe high over his head. "I will kneel perfectly still here in this hall, and he can strike me a single blow. Only he must swear that twelve months and a day from now

he will come to my place, where I will return the blow."

Well, you could have heard a cloak-pin drop. There wasn't a single taker. Maybe the other knights all knew more than I did, because it didn't sound too bad a deal to me. I mean, it was pretty obvious that if you knocked off his head in one go, he wouldn't be there twelve months and a day from now.

While I was weighing up my chances, the Green Knight was gloating. "So much for the bravery of the Knights of the Round Table!" he said. He looked round the room, his green eyes flashing under bushy green eyebrows. "You're nothing but a lot of beardless children," he said. Now I don't know if I imagined it, but I thought he was looking at me.

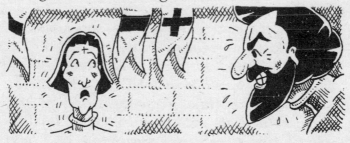

Anyway, by this time Uncle Arthur was on his feet, saying if nobody else was willing to take up the Green Knight's challenge he would do so himself. Now I'm sitting there, feeling really guilty for not having volunteered, especially after the mess I made over Lady Blamoure. So I jump up, shouting, "No, Sire," and next thing I hear is myself begging my uncle to let me fight the knight. "To wipe out my shame over killing a lady," I hear myself say.

I bet Uncle Arthur was relieved. It didn't take him long to say yes, that's for sure. So then the Green Knight asked me who I was, and I told him, Gawain, son of Lot, King of Orkney, and nephew to King Arthur. The Green Knight grinned and said, "Very good. Now step down here and I'll give you the axe. When you've had your go, I'll tell you who I am and where you can find me twelve months from now." Well, I could hardly back down at that point with everyone watching, so I stepped into the centre of the hall and took the axe from him.

He was a real show-off. He made out he was making everything easy for me. He knelt down, and bowed his head, which still meant his neck was about the height of my shoulders. Then he parted his green hair, so that the green skin of his neck was bare. I thought to myself, this is one I'd better not miss. I took the axe in both hands, raised it over my head, and brought it down as hard as I could on that green neck of his. The blade sliced clean through his neck in a single stroke and struck the stone floor of the hall so hard that sparks flew. A great cheer went up as his head rolled on to the floor.

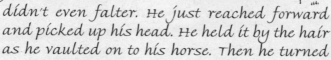

I've done it! I thought.

But little did I know...

The knight didn't fall down dead. He didn't even falter. He just reached forward and picked up his head. He held it by the hair as he vaulted on to his horse. Then he turned and faced me and, is this creepy, or what – the head spoke!!!!!

"See that you keep your oath!" he said. "I am the Knight of the Green Chapel. I live in the Forest of Wirral. There you must find me twelve months from now, unless you choose to break your knightly oath!"

With that he rode out of the hall, his head under his arm. Everyone just stared. Then they all turned and looked at me. Uncle Arthur called for more mead, and everyone started to loosen up and talk and laugh.

It's all very well for them. They don't have to

go for the return match a year from now. Just my luck to challenge a knight who can put his head back on after it's been cut off! I wonder how he did it? Still, a year is a long time. With any luck I may be killed in a joust or a battle before then.

Michaelmas Day – 9 months later

Still alive. I'm now $23\frac{1}{4}$. They say time flies as you get older. It must be true. I have never known a year go past as fast as this one. Soon I'll have to go up north to the Forest of Wirral on my warhorse Gringalet to find the Knight of the Green Chapel. I wish I had a lady whose favour I could wear in my helmet, though it is probably just as well that I don't because I don't think I'll live to see the lady again. Just my luck!

15th December

I'm really fed up. I've been travelling for weeks. Wales is horrible, all wild mountains and forest. The weather is cold and wet, it's dark by mid-afternoon and my armour leaks. Gringalet is lame, and I think I have athlete's foot, unless it is gangrene (Must be the thought of that green  giant. Ha, ha!). Every day I have to fight off robbers and bandits. I wish I'd never risen to the Green Knight's challenge. Maybe I'll get lucky and be eaten by wolves before I find the Forest of Wirral.

23rd December

Have found the Forest of Wirral (unfortunately!), over the River Dee from Wales, but there's no sign of the Knight of the Green Chapel.

24th December

What a relief! Thought I was never going to get to the end of marsh and mire. All of a sudden I came out of the woods, and there was a castle, with lawns in front and oak trees on either side. I rode up to the gate and shouted to the gatekeeper that I was from King Arthur's court, and pray would he tell his lord that I was here.

Uncle Arthur's name certainly opens doors. Next thing I knew the fellow opened the drawbridge and suddenly there were squires and serving men helping me dismount, and leading Gringalet away to the stables. Then I was taken in to meet the Lord of the Castle, who  seems very nice. I think I may have met him before somewhere, but I can't think where. He is 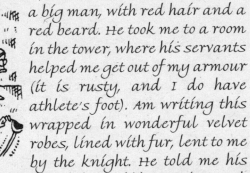 a big man, with red hair and a red beard. He took me to a room in the tower, where his servants helped me get out of my armour (it is rusty, and I do have athlete's foot). Am writing this wrapped in wonderful velvet robes, lined with fur, lent to me by the knight. He told me his name when I arrived, but I didn't quite catch it. It seems rude to ask again. With a bit of luck someone else will call him by his name, and then I'll know what it is.

25th December

The red-bearded knight did me proud last night. I had a five-course meal and plenty to drink. The knight and his court all raised their goblets and drank a toast to me. And I met the knight's lady. Eat your heart out, Uncle Arthur, she is even more beautiful than Aunty Gwin.

We all stayed up till two in the morning. When I went up to bed there was a goblet of hot, spicy mead waiting for me. I don't get this sort of treatment at home.

Wish Eleanor could see me now.

28th December

Three wonderful days of feasting and merriment have gone by! I'm not being big-headed, but I think the Lady of the Castle has a bit of a thing about me. She keeps sitting by me, and singing love songs on her lute. Just as well Eleanor's not here to see. Although it might make her realize I'm quite a catch!

Today I told the knight that I ought to be going about my High Quest (this is how knights talk, I'm really getting the hang of it). I explained that I have to find the Green Chapel by New Year's Day.

At this the Lord of the Castle laughed and said the chapel was only a two-hour ride away, and he would send someone with me to show me the way, so I could easily stay with him another few days. Naturally I said yes.

The Lord of the Castle is going hunting tomorrow, but I'm still tired from my journey, so he told me to stay at home and rest. Then he said something really weird. He said we should make a bargain. He'll give me whatever he manages to bring home from the hunt, and in return, I'm to give him, "whatever may come to me here in the castle". Can't imagine what he's talking about, but I said yes anyway, just to be polite.

29th December

Slept in, when I woke the lord had gone off hunting, and his lady was in my bedroom! At first I thought it was a dream, which was very nice, but then I realized

I wasn't imagining it. She really was sitting on my bed! The things she was saying! It's very difficult being an honourable knight when ladies are out to lead you astray. Then, if you please, she said I'd been very rude. It wasn't good manners to spend so much time with a lady and not give her a kiss. I felt like asking her who was spending time with whom. I mean, she was the one who came into my bedroom. Anyway, what about her old man? Doesn't she understand that I'm longing to kiss her but I have to do right by him as well?

In the end I said if she commanded me to, of course, I would ask a kiss of her. So she kissed me. Wow!

Now I'm wondering what I'm going to do about the bargain when the Lord of the Castle comes home.

Bedtime

The Lord of the Castle had a good day's hunting. He came home weighed down with dead deer, and just like he said he would, he gave them all to me. I'd been thinking maybe I should forget what had come my way. After all, I don't want to come between a knight and his wife. Then I remembered my knightly honour, and thought I'd better come clean. So I put my hands on his shoulders and kissed him, and told him that a kiss was the only thing which had come to me that day.  He didn't seem to think it was as odd as I did, but he did ask me where I'd got my "prize" from. So I just smiled and said that it wasn't part of the bargain to tell him that, which I thought was pretty clever.

Another huge meal this evening. I shall have to go on a diet when I go home. If I go home.

30th December

I think the sooner I leave here the better. Today the Lord of the castle went hunting wild boar, and his wife came hunting me!!!! I woke up to find her sitting on my bed again. She gave me two long kisses, and at the time I wasn't a bit sorry.

When her lord came home I was a bit worried, but he didn't ask any awkward questions, just said I would be rich if we went on like this, him giving me all his hunting spoils and only getting a kiss or two in return.

I think it's pretty impressive that I haven't done anything wrong with the lady, considering I'm going to my doom the day after tomorrow. The Lord of the Castle reckons I should have a lie-in till noon as it's the last day of my holiday. He's going fox-hunting.

31st December

Didn't sleep a wink all night, kept thinking about the Green Knight. Must have dozed off towards morning, 'cos when I woke the Lady of the Castle was in my bedroom again, kissing me on the mouth, and telling me I was a lazy so-and-so. I must say, she was looking drop-dead gorgeous, long hair falling down around her face. It was all I could do not to run off with her. She called me a man of ice and wanted to know if I had a girlfriend back at Camelot. I said no, and reminded her that she had a husband, and he'd been very good to me, and for the sake of my knighthood and the glory of Logres I couldn't betray her husband. Then she got really nasty, but I rose

above it and didn't answer back. Finally she turned all sweet and loving again, and told me I was a true and noble knight, and asked for a present to remember me by. There's no stopping some women. I couldn't think of anything to give her, I haven't got any luggage with me. Next thing I knew, she was giving me a green lace from her belt and asking me to wear it for her sake. I told her I couldn't

wear her favour, it would mean I was her knight, which obviously I can't be. (Though come to think of it, old Lancelot doesn't seem to have a problem with this sort of thing.) Then the lady told me that the lace was magic, and that if I wore it, I couldn't be killed.

Well, what would you do? I reckon I need all the help I can get. Maybe it'll work, and if it doesn't, no one will know anyway, 'cos I'll be dead.

When the Lord of the Castle came home I gave him three kisses, but I didn't let on about the lace.

The wind has got up and the rain is lashing down. It's a terrible thing to face death at such a young age.

1st January

Didn't sleep a single wink. Up at dawn. Tied the green lace around my waist under my armour. Don't suppose it will do any good, but you never know. It can't hurt.

Gringalet has been well fed. The squires brought him out and helped me to mount, and I said goodbye to the Lord of the Castle and his lady wife.

I told them that if I lived I would reward them for their kindness to me, but that I didn't expect to see another sunrise. Then I rode over the drawbridge, with a squire as a guide. Weather terrible — trees dripping, wind moaning. After a couple of hours' riding through dark woods, we came to a valley, and the squire warned me not to go on. He said the Green Knight is a terrible, cruel man, who kills everyone who passes his way. He said if I did a bunk now he wouldn't rat on me. Why is everyone always tempting me, that's what I want to know?

Anyway, I rose to the challenge. I told him I couldn't think of running off. I would be a coward, and unworthy of my knighthood.

More fool you, said the squire. He turned back, and there I was on my own. So much for taking me to the Green Chapel. I hadn't a clue where it was. I must have ridden on for another hour, and then I knew I was in the right place because I heard the most terrible sound. It was as if someone was sharpening a blade on a stone. I rode towards it, and then I saw the chapel. It didn't look much like a chapel, more like a moss-covered mound. What a place to die, I thought. I shouted out that I was there, and someone with a very deep voice shouted back to wait a minute, and that when his weapon was ready, "You shall have that which I promised you!"

So I dismounted from Gringalet and tied him to a tree and waited. Soon the knight appeared.

He was as huge and as green as ever. He came down the hill from the chapel and jumped over the stream with his axe in his hand.

"Welcome, Gawain," he said. "Now's the moment when I return that blow you struck me at Camelot. Take your helmet off, and get ready!"

This looked like the end for me but I did as he said. He raised his axe, and I heard it whistle as he brought it down. I must have flinched because he stopped it in mid-air.

"Ha!" he said. "So much for Gawain the Brave! When you cut off my head I never flinched."

"Maybe it's because I can't pick up my head and stick it back on again like you," I told him. I felt like a bald chicken kneeling there with my bare neck.

"Hark at you!" shouted the Green Knight, whirling his axe again. This time I didn't flinch, but he still stopped in mid-air and he told me I was doing well. I was thoroughly fed up by this time. He was playing games with me, and it was torture.

"Why don't you stop talking and get on with it?" I asked him.

"I shall," he said. "Pull your hood aside a bit more, I'm going to strike my hardest."

This really is it, I thought, as I heard him whirling his axe over his head once more. Next  thing I felt the axe connect with my neck and saw drops of blood in the snow! I jumped away from him, grabbed my helmet, and drew my sword.

"You had your chance and you muffed it," I yelled. "Now I'm going to defend myself!"

But the Green Knight wouldn't fight. He just stood there leaning on his axe.

"Yes, you kept your word, Gawain," he said, "and I'm not going to strike you again. I could have cut off your head the way you cut off mine, but I didn't want to." Then, blow me down, it turns out he's only the Lord of the Castle where I've just been staying! He knows all about me and his wife. The first two blows were for the kisses she gave me, which I told him about, and the third one, when he cut my neck, was because I hadn't told him about the green lace.

When he said that, I didn't know where to put myself. I went bright red. He just laughed, and told me I could keep the lace, I'd done very well. I asked him who he was, and how he

managed not to die when he was beheaded, and why he was both the Lord of the Castle and the Knight of the Green Chapel. He told me his name — he is called Sir Bertilak, Knight of the Lake — and that it was Auntie Morgan (le Fay) who turned him green and sent him to test the Knights of the Round Table to see if all the good things people say about them are true. Bertilak invited me back to his place, but I didn't feel much like it, so I sent my best regards to his wife, and said I had to get going.

I'm riding back to Camelot. They'll be very surprised to see me. One thing's for sure — I bet nobody's had a better adventure than me this year. What's the betting I get to be centre stage next year, and tell my story? I wonder if they'll believe me?!

FANTASTIC FACTS 4: THE CELTS

1 The Green Knight, or the Green Man, was a Celtic figure who was probably a symbol of nature and fertility. He has lived on long after Celtic times, carved as a gargoyle into medieval churches, along with saints and monsters – and he survives today as a common name for pubs.

2 In their heyday the Celtic tribes ruled the whole of Europe. Then the Romans became very powerful and drove them out to the western fringes – the British Isles, Ireland and western France, which was known as Gaul. But their beliefs and customs weren't so easily defeated – some of them continue to this very day.

3 The Celts left no written records. As a result almost everything we know about them was written by their enemies – the Romans who conquered them, and later, the Christian monks who disapproved of their pagan ways. This doesn't mean that the Celts were ignorant. They just passed on their knowledge from one generation to the next by word of mouth.

4 The Celts were the first iron-using tribes and were fantastic metalworkers. Wonderful Celtic cauldrons, jewellery, swords, flagons and armour, which they beat, smelted and decorated thousands of years ago, have been found. Some were in the graves of their princes and princesses – so the Celts must have believed their nobles would need wealth and weapons after they died. Other remains have been found at the bottom of lakes. Maybe they considered these lakes sacred, and offered their best ornaments to them. This may be the reason why Arthur got his sword from the Lady of the Lake – she was just throwing one back!

5 Despite their brilliant metalwork, the knight in shining armour is not a Celtic figure. Many Celtic tribes fought naked – that way they were more nimble than their enemies (so long as they didn't land on anything sharp!). Often they painted themselves with woad, a blue dye they made from plants. This made them look wild and fierce, but it wasn't the only reason they did it. Wounds get infected by dirty clothing – and modern scientists have discovered that woad is antiseptic.

6 Celtic warriors liked nothing better than a good fight. The Cimri, a tribe of Celts from Germany, beat the Romans in France – and then tobogganed down the Alps into Italy on their shields. They weren't after plunder – they burned the Romans' clothes and armour, and threw all their gold and silver in the river. If an enemy was too tired to give them a good fight, they would stop the battle. But when Celtic warriors retreated, their women would send them back to fight some more. Then if the men wouldn't fight, the women killed themselves and their children.

7 It was normal for Celts to foster each other's children. Boys were not allowed to be with their fathers until they were fighting men themselves, and even then were supposed to keep out of the fathers' sight in public. Children who were fostered together considered themselves brothers and sisters. So when Arthur was spirited off by Merlin, and Lancelot was taken by the Lady of the Lake, it was considered quite normal.

8 Celtic queens and Celtic priestesses were powerful people; even women who were not queens were allowed to marry who they liked, to own property, and to leave an unhappy marriage taking their property with them. So women got a much better deal in Celtic society than they did later, when the Church became powerful.

9 Celtic priests and priestesses were known as Druids. Their religion forbade them to write down their teachings, which were passed on orally (by word-of-mouth). To do this they memorized hundreds of verses – it took students of Druidism about 20 years to learn them all. Ordinary people were gobsmacked by this, as well as by their other powers of healing and prophecy. Druids believed in reincarnation, and honoured nature as being sacred. They studied the movement of the stars, and held discussions about life, the universe and everything.

10 Even people who didn't like the Celts commented on their gift of the gab. One Roman writer said the Celts considered storytelling an even more important skill than fighting – because they knew that words were more powerful than swords.

Can you guess which of the following traditions date back to Celtic times?

1 Fireworks on Bonfire Night
2 Ducking for apples on Hallowe'en
3 Making turnip lanterns
4 Exchanging Christmas presents
5 Nativity plays
6 Kissing under the mistletoe
7 Making straw dollies at harvest time
8 Easter eggs
9 Going away for a summer holiday
10 Poppy Day

Answers:

Numbers **2, 3, 6, 7** and **8** date from Celtic times.

2 Ducking for apples is thought to be part of an ancient Druid ritual. Remember, Avalon was the land of apples, and the Lady of the Lake lived under water.

3 Turnip lanterns probably represent the severed heads of conquered enemies! The Celts were said to be head-hunters and cannibals who boiled up the bodies of their victims in enormous cauldrons! This is what a Roman writer called Diodorus Siculus wrote in a World History in the 1st century BC said: *When the Celts kill enemies in battle they cut off their heads and attach them to the necks of their horses ... They soak the heads of their most illustrious enemies in cedar oil and keep them carefully in a chest to show off to strangers.*

6 Mistletoe was sacred to the Druids, and they decorated their shrines with it. We also know the Celts had rave parties around the midwinter solstice – popular even then.

7 Some people still make straw dollies today, but they're nothing like the original Celtic straw man. He was a wicker giant, but he was hollow, so the Celts could stuff their enemies inside and set fire to them. At least, that's what the Romans said. The Celts also went in for bonfires but not fireworks. They lit them at Beltane, their spring festival – 1 May.

LEGEND 5: MERLIN GOES MISSING

One of the most mysterious stories of all the Arthurian legends concerns the disappearance of Merlin. Why did he disappear? Where did he go? Here, Sir Muldevaine and Dame Sculliana from the O(therworld)-Files go time-travelling to attempt to solve the mystery in Legend number 5.

Voices in the wind
The story of the disappearance of Merlin

1 The courtyard of a medieval castle, daytime.
Agent Muldevaine, dressed in medieval doublet and hose, is tightening the saddle girth on his horse, when into the courtyard strides Agent Sculliana, her long black coat flapping open over a medieval dress. On

her head she wears a tall-pointed medieval hat with a veil.

Sculliana: Hey, Muldevaine. What's with all this glam gear?

Muldevaine looks round. A small smile plays on his lips as he looks her up and down.

Muldevaine: You're asking me? Have you taken a look in the mirror recently?

Sculliana: (*She looks down at her clothes.*) Wow, am I dreaming this?

Muldevaine: I don't know. I thought I was.

Sculliana: The guy at the gate said this was Camelot.

Muldevaine: That's right. Year 1250. I have to say I'm surprised to see you. I never thought you'd make it across the centuries.

Sculliana: I came 'cos I got a call from you on my mobile. Missing person case you said?

Muldevaine: That's right, some guy called Merlin. He was last seen at a summer festival. Pentecost, I think it's called. Something to do with—

Sculliana: I know what Pentecost is, Muldevaine. It's a Church festival.

Muldevaine: Yeah. Well, that was the last time the guy was seen. Then he disappeared into the forest and hasn't been seen since. He's not just any guy, Sculliana. He's the Chief Druid round here.

Sculliana: That's some sort of priest, right?

Muldevaine: Yeah, and the rest. He's a seer, clairvoyant and magician, and he's just vanished into thin air. A knight called Bagdemagus reckons he's been buried alive. He heard him moaning and wailing.

Sculliana: OK, so I guess we go out there and take a look.

Muldevaine: *(indicating a grey mare, standing saddled nearby)* There's your palfrey.

Sculliana: My what? You expect me to ride that thing?

CUT TO
2 Glade in the woods, evening
The light is fading, and the branches of the trees are whipping in the wind. In the middle of the glade there is a large flat stone, like a tombstone, except it is wedged against a rock.

Sculliana: Is this the place?

Muldevaine: Shh! Listen.

Sculliana: What?

Muldevaine: Can't you hear it?

Sculliana: Muldevaine, you know me. When it comes to the music of the spheres, I'm tone deaf.

Muldevaine dismounts from his horse and puts his ear to the crack between rock and stone.

Merlin: (voice over) Woe is me! Woe is me!

Muldevaine: There is someone there! (*He cups his hands, and directs his voice into the crack.*) Merlin? Is that you? Can you hear me? Are you injured, Merlin?
No answer.

Sculliana: You're talking to yourself, Muldevaine. There's no one in there.
Muldevaine shakes his head.

Muldevaine: Merlin, do you hear me? We're going to get you out of there. We'll get some proper lifting gear, and have this stone moved away in no time.

Merlin: (v/o) No one can release me but the one who put me here!

Muldevaine: Who's that, Merlin?

Merlin: (v/o) Nim-u-ë. Nim-u-ë.

Muldevaine: (*standing up*) I thought as much.

Sculliana: What?

Muldevaine: He said Nimuë shut him up here, and she's the only one who can release him.

Sculliana: He *said* that? Are you certain? Because all I could hear was the wind.

Muldevaine: I heard him, Sculliana. Come on, we have to find Nimuë. (*calling*) Don't worry, we'll be back, Merlin.

Muldevaine remounts his horse, rides out of the glade. Sculliana follows.

CUT TO
3 A road beside a river, the next evening
Sir Muldevaine and Dame Sculliana are riding side-by-side.

Sculliana: So who is this Nimuë?

Muldevaine: She's one powerful lady. Some sort of priestess. She has a number of aliases: Vivienne, Ninian and Neneve. Some people say she is really the Lady of the Lake. She lives in the Otherworld, or she used to. Just recently she seems to be in this world quite a lot. You could say she's picked up a lot of Merlin's business.

Sculliana: What do you mean?

Muldevaine: I mean all the prophecy, communicating with the Otherworld on behalf of the people at the court of King Arthur. Since Merlin vanished, Nimuë's taken over that side of things.

Sculliana: You think that's why she got rid of him?

Muldevaine: It's possible. There are a number of other stories about her. One is that she was in love with Merlin, and he wasn't interested, so she tried to poison him. The other tale they tell about her is—

But as he is speaking a cloaked figure steps out from behind a tree into their path. Muldevaine and Sculliana rein their horses. Muldevaine pulls his gun and holds it, two-handed, pointing at the figure.

Nimuë: Put that gun away. It will not work here in Logres.

Nimuë lets the hood of her cloak drop, revealing a pale face and long dark hair, hanging loose. She has a band around her brow.

Muldevaine: You're Nimuë?

Nimuë: (*She nods.*) And you are Agents Sir Muldevaine and Dame Sculliana.

Sculliana: How do you know our names?

Nimuë: (*with a mysterious smile*) Such things are child's play to the Lady of the Lake.

Muldevaine: We have a few questions for you, Ms Nimuë. You were a friend of Merlin, is that right?

Nimuë: *(another mysterious smile)* I am a friend of his.

Sculliana: Are you saying that he's still alive?

Nimuë: The soul does not die.

Muldevaine: We're not talking about the soul, Ms Nimuë. We want to know about his body. We have reason to believe he's been kidnapped.

Nimuë: Who could kidnap Merlin? He would put a spell on you as soon as look at you.

Muldevaine: Rumour has it you cast quite a spell on him yourself.

Nimuë: No. Who told you that?

Muldevaine: Just about everyone at King Arthur's court.

Nimuë: Merlin was too old for love.

Muldevaine: Yeah, they say that too. That he made a fool of himself running after a beautiful young creature like yourself...

Nimuë smiles again, and sits down by the river. She holds a twig which she trails in the fast-running water.

Muldevaine: They say you promised that if he told you all his magic you would love him.

Nimuë: (*looking up, lazy and flirtatious*) People say many things, Agent Muldevaine.

Muldevaine: But it is true, isn't it, that Merlin disguised himself as a young squire in order to win your heart?
Nimuë doesn't reply.

Muldevaine: They say that he called up an enchanted forest, a whole world, with knights and ladies dancing and singing for your delight. There was also a river, and a place beyond that where you could go and have anything you wanted. But that wasn't enough for you, was it Ms Nimuë? You wanted to be able to conjure up such things for yourself.

Nimuë: Is that so surprising?

Muldevaine: So you led him on because you wanted to know his secrets.

Nimuë: What secrets can Merlin have that the Lady of the Lake does not already know?

Muldevaine: The secret of how to imprison a man in thin air.

Nimuë: No. No one can do that, not even Merlin.

Muldevaine: Is Sir Bagdemagus right, Ms Nimuë? Is Merlin imprisoned for all time beneath that stone?

Nimuë: There is no one beneath that stone, Agent Muldevaine.

Muldevaine: Oh yes there is, I heard him.

Nimuë: You heard nothing but the wind. Agent Sculliana knows that.

Sculliana: So where is Merlin if he isn't there?

Nimuë: You should go and ask Merlin's sister, Ganieda. Queen to King Rodarch of Cumbria.

As she speaks, Nimuë steps out on to the surface of the river, and walks away from them into the dusk.

Muldevaine: Come back. We aren't done yet...

Sculliana: She walked on water! Did you see that, Muldevaine? It's not possible. (*She puts her hand to her head.*) This place is really getting to me.

Muldevaine: I'm going after her.
He wades into the water.

Sculliana: You'll get wet!
She watches him go.

Sculliana: (*calling after him*) Hey, Muldevaine!

Muldevaine: (*looking back*) Yeah?

Sculliana: I'm going to check out the sister. I'll be in touch.

CUT BETWEEN
4 Turret room in castle in northern England and banqueting hall at Camelot
Sculliana stands at a window from which she can look down on the courtyard below. In her hand she has a mobile phone. She punches out Muldevaine's number.

CUT TO
Muldevaine at dinner with a number of King Arthur's knights and their ladies. His mobile phone rings, he takes it out of his jerkin pocket.

Muldevaine: Muldevaine.

Sculliana: (v/o) Hi, Muldevaine. Where are you? Did you catch up with Nimuë?

Muldevaine: No. She vanished like – I don't know what. One minute she was there and the next she was gone. Then the most beautiful white deer crossed my path—

Sculliana: A white deer?

Muldevaine: Yeah, I've never seen one before. It was dark by then and it just seemed to glow in the darkness.

Sculliana: Well, that's very interesting, Muldevaine, because I've been talking to a few people. Apparently the white deer is associated with Nimuë. The first time Nimuë appeared at Arthur's court, it was in pursuit of a white deer.

Muldevaine: Yeah, well, I don't see where that gets us. Merlin's still under the rock, and Nimuë's vanished into thin air.

Sculliana: Now that's where you're wrong. Merlin's not under the rock.

Muldevaine: He's not under the rock? You've found him?

Sculliana: Not exactly. But there have been quite a few sightings of him. If you ask me he's lucky he's not on a murder charge himself. You'd better get yourself up here to King Rodarch's place. I'll tell you all about it then.

CUT TO

5 Gardens of King Rodarch's palace, day
Muldevaine and Sculliana are walking in the gardens.

Sculliana: Merlin's sister, Ganieda, heard that he was living in the Caledonian Forest north of here. He'd witnessed a terrible battle and he was mad with grief at all the pointless killing. So she brought Merlin to court – but he had to be chained, he was so crazy. Ganieda tried to persuade him to take his wife back to the forest to look after him, but he said no. He said he wanted his wife to marry again. Then when she did, he killed her and her bridegroom with a pair of stag's antlers.

Muldevaine: That's why you said Merlin should be on a murder charge.

Sculliana: That's right.

Muldevaine: So where is Merlin now?

Sculliana: He's in the forest. Queen Ganieda has promised to take us there tonight.

CUT TO
6 Hart Fell Forest, night
It is a moonlit night. Queen Ganieda leads Muldevaine and Sculliana through shadowy thickets until they come to a clearing. There is a house with seventy doors and windows of glass. They approach quietly. Ganieda peers through a window, and beckons to Muldevaine and Sculliana to come and look. They do so. We take their point of view, and see Merlin, now a very old man, looking up through the windows of his roof at the stars. Around him are charts of the heavens.

Sculliana: Does he do this every night?

Ganieda: Yes.

Muldevaine: Looks like a lonely life.

Sculliana: Does it? I'd say he has a visitor.

Still from their point of view, we see another old man approaching Merlin's door.

Muldevaine: Who's that?

Ganieda: Taliessin. King Arthur's court poet. He visits Merlin every night. They plot the movements of the stars, and set the world to rights.

Merlin and Sculliana look at each other.

Sculliana: (*with a shrug*) Looks like there's no missing person after all, Muldevaine. Time we went back to Baltimore.

Muldevaine: So who was that I heard crying in the rocks, Sculliana?

Sculliana: It was the wind, Muldevaine. You heard the wind.

CUT TO
7 Glade in the woods, morning
This is the same glade where Muldevaine heard Merlin. The wind is blowing, and above it we can just hear the same cry as before.

Merlin: (v/o) Oh wo-o-o-e! Wooo-ooo-e is me!

THE END
CUE THEME MUSIC AND CREDITS.

FANTASTIC FACTS 5: TIME AND PLACE IN ARTHURIAN LEGEND

Dame Sculliana knew that Pentecost was a Church festival, but do you? What about Michaelmas? When was it? What was it celebrating?

Here are the top ten dates of the medieval year. They are almost all Christian festivals celebrating Jesus and the Christian saints. In fact our word "holiday" originally meant "holy day". These were the only days people had off work.

1. *Christmas Day*: 25 December, celebration of the birth of Jesus Christ in a manger.
2. *Twelfth Night*: 12 days on from that, surprise, surprise. Time when the three wise men came to visit baby Jesus.
3. *Lent*: the six weeks before Easter when you're meant to give up chocolate or watching telly. Why? To remind you of the 40 days Jesus spent fasting (not eating) in the wilderness. In medieval times, people really did fast. That's when the custom of Pancake Day began. People made pancakes on Shrove Tuesday to use up all their leftovers before Lent.
4. *Palm Sunday:* The Sunday before Easter and the day when Jesus rode into Jerusalem

on an ass, and people lined the roads waving palm branches to welcome him.

5. ***Maundy Thursday***: Thursday before Easter: the night when Jesus ate with his disciples for the last time (The Last Supper) and washed their feet. For many years, people had a good laugh watching royalty and posh people wash their feet (hope they didn't smell too much), in memory of this day. The rich would also give out clothes and food on this day. The custom (just) survives when the Queen gives out "Maundy money" to Chelsea pensioners on Maundy Thursday every year.

6. ***Easter***: Consists of *Good Friday*, which commemorates the day when Jesus was put to death by the Romans and the following Sunday, Easter Day, when the Church celebrates the resurrection (rising from the dead) of Jesus Christ.

Easter is a "lunar" festival (which means it's related to the moon). And no, this does not mean that you can stay out late and howl at the moon. This means that Easter doesn't fall on the same day every year. It's based on the phases of the moon, and follows the first full moon of the Spring Equinox. Got that? Good.

7. ***Pentecost***: Seventh Sunday after Easter Sunday. Day when the Holy Spirit descended on the followers of Jesus and filled them with light, fire and courage. They found themselves speaking in languages they

did not understand – but other people did. Also known as: Whitsunday; Whitsuntide.

8. **Midsummer Day**: 24 June. Known as St John's Day by the medieval Church, although like Christmas it was probably an old pagan festival. If you think of the year as a circle, then Midsummer Day would be a point directly opposite Christmas Day. This was a very important ancient festival, celebrated at Stonehenge and other stone circles around Europe. Lots of people still think of Midsummer Day as a day when magic is in the air and strange things happen.

9. **Lammas**: 1 August. Also known as Harvest Festival, originally celebrated with loaves of bread made from the first ripe corn of the harvest. People still give thanks at this time of year for the food we have to eat, but not many of us farm corn anymore, so you'll often see a few tins of beans in the church!

10. **Michaelmas**: Feast of St Michael, 29 September. St Michael is a big hero in the last book of the New Testament, the Book of Revelation, when he leads the forces of the good against the forces of evil. Michaelmas is still used to describe the Autumn term in some universities and in the Law Courts – and the small purple daisies with yellow centres that flower in early Autumn are called Michaelmas daisies.

May Day was also an important date in the Arthurian calendar, though not a church festival: On 1 May, the Queen and her ladies went out gathering hawthorn blossom, also known as "may".

MERLIN'S MANY HOMES

There are Merlin's Caves at Chislehurst in Kent, and at Tintagel in Cornwall. There's a Merlin's Well at Alderley Edge near Manchester, Merlin's Rock at Mousehole in Cornwall, and Carmarthen (Caer Myrrdin), the name of a town in Wales actually means "Merlin's Hill". There are Merlin's Tombs at Marlborough in Wiltshire, Mynned Myrddin (a mountain in Wales), and Comper in France, and a Merlin's Grave at Drumelzier in Scotland. Hart Fell, near Moffat in Scotland is supposed to be the site of the observatory or "mad prophet's lair".

So how did Merlin get around so much without an executive jet?

One possibility is that Merlin was not one person, but several. Merlin means Druid, or perhaps Chief Druid, so it may be a bit like thinking the words Pope or Archbishop always refer to the one person.

But people did cover huge distances on foot and on horseback. They were used to it, and a good walker could average 40 kilometres (25 miles) a day. That's four days from London to Birmingham, and another eight from Manchester to Carlisle.

And we still don't know the truth about what happened to him!

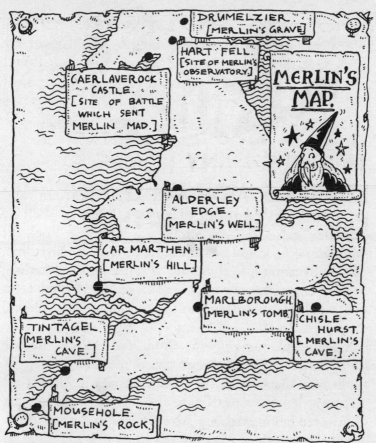

DRUMELZIER
[MERLIN'S GRAVE]

HART FELL
[SITE OF MERLIN'S OBSERVATORY.]

CAERLAVEROCK CASTLE.
[SITE OF BATTLE WHICH SENT MERLIN MAD.]

MERLIN'S MAP.

ALDERLEY EDGE.
[MERLIN'S WELL.]

CARMARTHEN.
[MERLIN'S HILL.]

MARLBOROUGH.
[MERLIN'S TOMB.]

TINTAGEL
[MERLIN'S CAVE.]

CHISLE- HURST.
[MERLIN'S CAVE.]

MOUSEHOLE.
[MERLIN'S ROCK.]

Did you know…?

When the Normans invaded Britain in 1066 they brought prefabricated wooden castles over with them. This meant they were able to build strongholds all over the country very quickly. Once they were settled, they replaced them with the stone keeps and castles of medieval legend.

LEGEND 6: MORGAN LE FAY PLOTS AGAINST ARTHUR

Why did Morgan le Fay hate King Arthur so much? No one really knows. Perhaps he was just too big for his boots. Or perhaps she was angry because he had used the old Celtic rules to get into power, but then refused to abide by them.

Then again, some people think that Arthur and his father Uther Pendragon were really the same person. If that's true, Queen Igrayne wasn't Arthur's mother at all – she was his first wife. There are stories that talk about Guinevere being Arthur's *second* wife. So maybe it was Arthur, not Uther, who pushed Morgan's dad aside to marry Igrayne. Then when Guinevere came along, he dumped her. This would have made Igrayne's daughter Morgan pretty angry!

Whatever the reason, there are plenty of stories where Morgan tries to bring Arthur down. Legend number six is in the form of letters that Morgan might have written to her sister Gausie. Gausie is Morgause, Queen of Orkney. Uri is Morgan's husband, Uriens, and Wayne is her son, Owaine.

MORGAN MIXES IT

Dearest Gausie,

Guess what? By the time you get this, that upstart Arthur will be finished for ever! I have cast the most wonderful spell. This time there will be no mistakes. His time has come!

I got the idea when I found out Uri was planning a weekend away with the boys — a hunting trip with Arthur and Sir Accolon. As you know, Acco has been in love with me for years. This was a fine chance — Arthur alone with two guys who'd die for me.

ACCO AND URI

After I waved goodbye to poor, stupid Uri, I changed into a deer and sped before them to the Welsh forest. I led them to a lake... and on it a smart little barge with silken sails glided to the sandy shore and beached itself... as if by chance! Do I need to tell you, dearest Gausie, that lake and barge were all part of my spell?

The sun was setting; the lads were miles from home. Of course, they went on board the barge. As the barge slid away from the shore, twelve pretty young girls brought out food, wine and roses and served it by torchlight. Six more sang and played on dulcimers. Truly, Gausie, I'd thought of everything to keep them happy. In fact, I actually thought I'd gone a bit over the top. But no, these dopey men did not suspect a thing!

When they were far gone with all the wine and food and soothing music, the girls led the men below, each to a bed so soft, so warm, so sweet, that in seconds all three were out like lights.

How I laughed. I stood there – invisible – in Arthur's cabin as he snored like a pig.

Then I did what I've wanted to do for many a year – I nicked his precious sword Excalibur, and its still more precious scabbard. Without it, his days are numbered! The first wound and he bleeds!

Now I had no more need for the barge – or Uri, come to that. He woke in his own bed at home, with me beside him, puzzled, poor fool, about how he came to be there, and worrying about "his lord, the King".

I was very kind to him. I did not tell him Arthur had woken far from home, in a dark and dripping dungeon, beside twenty other knights who for years have been prisoners of Sir Damas – I think

I've told you, Gausie, his daughter is one of my loyal ladies.

I sent this girl to speak to Arthur. She offered him a deal. He could leave the dungeon, and take the twenty knights with him – on one condition. He must fight in Sir Damas' name against a champion who would come that day.

Can you guess what I was up to, dearest Gausie? The champion was to be none other than Acco, armed with Excalibur! Did I tell you where I'd arranged for Acco to wake up? Right on the edge of a deep well – just in case he decided to be difficult.

Then, for good measure, there was an ugly little dwarf beside him, ready to push him in.

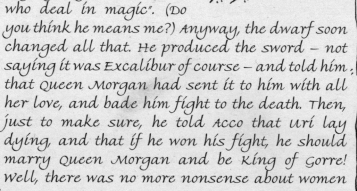

It was just as well I arranged that. Acco woke raging against "women who deal in magic". (Do you think he means me?) Anyway, the dwarf soon changed all that. He produced the sword – not saying it was Excalibur of course – and told him that Queen Morgan had sent it to him with all her love, and bade him fight to the death. Then, just to make sure, he told Acco that Uri lay dying, and that if he won his fight, he should marry Queen Morgan and be King of Gorre! Well, there was no more nonsense about women

who practise magic after that. Acco agreed at once.
The dwarf pulled him to safety and gave him
the scabbard and the sword.

So my dear, the stage is set. All we do now is
sit and wait for Acco and Arthur to finish this
once and for all. Knowing who has Excalibur
and, more important still, the scabbard, we know
which one will die!

Just think – thanks to my magic, your son,
the noble Gawain, will soon be King of Britain!
Which is just as it should be!

In haste, your loving sister,
Morgan

Two days later:

Dearest Gausie,

All is lost! You must destroy this letter, and
the last one too. My plan has failed, and all
because of Nimuë!

I can't believe I have
to write this news to you.
It was all going so well.
The morning of the fight,
the two men had their
visors down, so neither
recognized the other.
Arthur, of course, still
thought he had Excalibur.

108

He didn't know he was wearing a fake sword. When the fight started, poor Acco couldn't believe his luck. He landed blow after blow and Arthur bled – you should have seen the blood. Arthur was totally shocked. Bewildered. He staggered, fell, then stumbled up. His sword was broken clean in two.

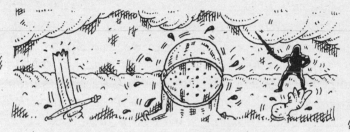

Then, just when it seemed that we had won, along came Nimuë. Meddling like the old man she has locked away. She must have cast a spell, for the scabbard slipped off Accolon. He stood there rooted to the spot and Arthur pounced. He strapped the scabbard to him. Next Accolon's sword twisted from his hand as if it had a life of its own! Arthur grabbed that, as well. He recognized Excalibur.

From that moment on, Arthur's bleeding stopped and Acco's wounds began to bleed. Arthur laid about him with Excalibur, and yelled at Accolon to yield. Acco refused – his honour would not let him.

"Then tell me who you are, brave knight," said Arthur.

So Acco raised his visor, and showed his face. Out of his stupid mouth poured the whole story. The dwarf, his love for me, my promise he should replace Uri. Then he asked – for  Arthur still had his visor down – who was this knight that Queen Morgana wanted dead?

When Arthur raised his visor and showed his face, Accolon fell upon his knees in shame and begged for mercy. I knew none of this until later, of course, for I was back at Camelot, so that no one should link me to Arthur's death. Besides, I had business there. If I was going to keep my promise and marry Acco, then Uri had to be got out of the way.

Would you believe it, Gausie, I was betrayed again! The girl I sent to fetch my dagger told our son, Wayne, my plot. He stopped me killing Uri. As for the things he said...

Next morning, the news came. Acco is dead of his wounds, while Arthur, curse him, is healing at an Abbey not far off.

I have to act quickly, sister, if I am to save my skin. At this very minute, my men are saddling up the horses. I am going to ride to Arthur, beg to see him, and swear that everything Acco told him was a lie...

In haste, my trusted Gausie. Please burn this letter!

Your loving sister,
Morgan

Two days later:
Dearest Gausie,

All is not lost after all! Arthur is still alive, but the scabbard is gone for ever. Here's how...

I reached the Abbey, talked my way in past the nuns. Put on a great show of Christian piety. I wished only to sit and watch beside my poor sick brother, I said.

Of course, they let me in. Arthur was asleep, his hand clutching his sword. Ah, but the scabbard lay on a chair by the door! Here was my chance! I sat there for a decent interval, but when I left that room, sister, I had the scabbard strapped beneath my cloak!

I rode on with my men-at-arms and ladies. No one knew the great treasure I was carrying. Then there was a terrific yell from the back of our group. Someone had spotted two knights riding hell for leather after us. I knew at once it must be Arthur and a friend. We spurred our horses, but it was no good, for they were gaining ground.

Luckily, we rode beside a deep lake of dark,  still water. I unfastened the scabbard, and threw it hard, right into the middle of the lake. It sank at once. Arthur will never set eyes on it again.

Then, because he was nearly upon us, and my ladies were squealing with fear, I cast a spell. The damsels, the men-at-arms and myself were changed immediately into vast rocks and boulders.

When Arthur and his man arrived, there was not a living soul in sight in that barren place, and only a last silent ripple on the lake. Arthur shuddered. He said that he could feel evil had been done, and magic was afoot. He searched and searched for us; but of course he found nothing. Finally he gave up and went home.

I have one last card up my sleeve, dear Gausie. To beg for mercy, and send gifts of peace. Do I need to tell you that the gifts will not be what they seem?

Hoping that my next letter will bring you news of the wretched upstart's death.

In haste, I am your loving sister,

Morgan

Three weeks later:

Dearest Gausie,

You must have heard what happened. A thousand curses on Nimuë!

I sent a girl to Arthur's court last night, bearing a cloak, set with gems as a present for the King. She told Arthur that I had been possessed by demons, and that it was the demons who had tried to kill him. They were now gone, and I had sent this cloak as a token of peace. Please would my brother wear it?

He never learns, poor Arthur. He stretched his hands to take my cloak, but Nimuë called out, "No! Not till you know it's safe!" She gave the mantle to my loyal damsel, and bade her try it on. The poor child protested, but Arthur, suspicious now, insisted.

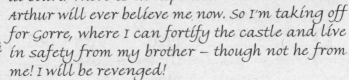

The girl is no more. As she drew the mantle round herself, flames ate her up. In moments, she was just a pile of ashes.

Sister, I am finished here at court. There is no hope that Arthur will ever believe me now. So I'm taking off for Gorre, where I can fortify the castle and live in safety from my brother – though not he from me! I will be revenged!

Your loving sister,
Morgan

TOP FACTS 6: ARTHUR'S SECRET SERVICE

King Arthur's Military Intelligence, A-MI5, must have had a hard time keeping tabs on the ladies of the Otherworld. Here are the ten best entries from their secret files. Six of them are about Morgan le Fay, but the rest are about other weird and wonderful Arthurian women.

TOP SECRET – **This means you!**
To be accessed only by people with Grade IV clearance.

Morgan le Fay

1 Youngest daughter of King Uther and Queen Igrayne. On the marriage of her two older sisters, Morgan was sent to school in a nunnery. Persistent rumours suggest that it was here that she discovered the black arts – pretending to know the future through contacting the dead – and developed her ability to cast spells and change her shape. However, it seems more likely that she came to these talents via the old Druid tradition. She was reputed to be a skilful healer. **Note:** Extremely dangerous and unpredictable; disloyal to the King. See also items 2-6.

2 10 February, AD 475. The kidnapping of Lancelot

Morgan was involved in the enchantment and kidnapping of Lancelot du Lac. She was one of four queens who came upon him while he was asleep. Some sort of row seems to have broken out between these  four women, probably about which of them he loved best. Queen of Northgalis reports that Morgan cast a spell on Lancelot, and kept him locked up in her castle until he declared his love for her. Lancelot refused to betray Queen G. **Note:** His escape was brought about by Agent X[*].

3 15 October, AD 481. Slander by shield

Morgan gave a shield to Sir Tristan on which was a painting of a king and queen, with a knight standing over them with a foot on each of their heads. The knight could be Sir Lancelot. Tristan wore  this shield at a tournament in the presence of Her Majesty, unaware

---

[*] A damsel at Morgan's castle acting as agent for HM Government.

of the meaning of the picture. **Note:** HM was greatly distressed by the incident, which was clearly intended by M. le F. to cause offence and scandal.

4 Christmas, AD 473. Morgan's change of shape (1)

An ugly old woman has newly appeared at the castle of Sir Bertilak on the Wirral Peninsula. First reports suggest this may be Morgan in one of her many transformations of shape.

Local rumours suggest that the Green Knight who appeared at Camelot this time last year and challenged the Knights of the Round Table may in fact be Sir Bertilak. **Note:** Suggest we ascertain whether he is an agent of M. le Fay, or if he has been enchanted by her. The latter explanation would explain his green skin, his size and his supernatural ability to function without his head.

5 The kidnapping of Alisander

Intelligence has reached us of a letter, allegedly from King Mark of Cornwall to Queen Morgan le Fay, asking her to, "set

the country on fire with enchantresses and dangerous knights" in order to capture his enemy, Alisander l'Orphelin. Alisander is now missing; when last seen, he was very badly wounded after a tournament.

Update: Alisander has surfaced in Camelot, claiming that he has been a prisoner of Morgan le Fay. He says that she kidnapped him after giving him a sleeping potion, and also claims that she healed his wounds with a magic ointment. Her intention had been to keep him with her for ever, but Alisander, who has a girlfriend, managed to escape.

6 Morgan's change of shape (2)

A strange cloud formation has been seen off the coast of Sicily, bringing stormy weather. Local soldiers say these clouds are none other than Morgan le Fay, and have given them the name "Fata Morgana". *

---

* The Normans, who invaded and ruled Sicily as well as Britain in the 11th century, really did believe these clouds were one of Queen Morgan's many changes of shape.

Top secret files: Miscellaneous females

7 Name unknown: She goes by the nickname "The White-haired Queen".

This is a woman of royal birth, elderly, but still a good-looker, who always dresses in white, with flowers in her hair. She lives with two other women, in a castle known as the "Castle of Maidens". Only widows, orphans, virgins or squires are allowed to live in this place. Rumours abound that this woman is none other than King Arthur's mother, Queen Igrayne.

When Uther died, Igrayne disappeared without trace. Locals say she brought all her gold and silver north with her, and built this castle on a rock. The two other queens are said to be Morgause and Clarrisant – her daughter and granddaughter. However, government spies observing a recent visit to the castle by Sir Gawain say that he did not recognize any of the three queens, even when they asked about his family. This seems odd, because if the rumours are true, these women would be his mother, his sister and his grandmother.

Although it seems unlikely this woman is who people say she is, she seems harmless. **Note:** It is possible that Gawain did know the three women, but knew that our agents were in the castle and so pretended not to recognize them. Discreet surveillance of both the castle and Sir Gawain should be continued.

8 Dame Brisen

Lady-in-waiting to Elaine of Carbonek and a small-time enchantress, responsible for causing L. du Lac to betray the Queen. Her mistress, Elaine, was put under a spell by Morgan which kept her stuck in a bath of scalding water for some years. She  was finally rescued by Lancelot du Lac – eyewitnesses say she was "naked as a needle" when he hauled her out. The girl, Elaine, fell for her rescuer, and persuaded Brisen to cast a spell so Lancelot would return her love. Brisen pulled it off, but her magic did not last. Daylight broke the spell, and when Lancelot opened the shutters he was horrified, and beat a hasty retreat. **Note:** Brisen maintains that the child born to Elaine nine months later is Lancelot's son. Could cause a few problems at court if news of this gets out.

9 A missing body

The body of a woman, aged about 25, has been reported missing from a mysterious unnamed castle. The corpse is thought to be Dindrane, sister of Sir Percival. Dindrane had been travelling with her brother Sir Bors and Sir Galahad in the quest of the Holy Grail. On arrival at this castle, they were hailed by a knight on patrol on the battlements who, seeing they had a woman with them, asked  if she was married or a maiden. When told she was a maiden, he said she must yield to "the custom of the castle", and fill a large dish with the blood of her right arm. Percival wanted to fight to protect her, but Dindrane said no. The blood was apparently needed to heal the lady of the castle who had been ill for many years. Dindrane then died of loss of blood, while the lady of the castle made a full recovery.

(Postscript added two years later.)

Forensic tests on the female body, which mysteriously reappeared when the knights seeking the Holy Grail reached the end of their Quest, suggest that this was Dindrane. The Grail knights buried the body with full ceremony as befitted a woman of rank.

Note: We have no intelligence as to how the body reached its new site, or what had happened to it in the meantime. Presents no danger as far as we know.

10 "The hideous damsel"

Name: Ragnell. Easily recognized. An eyewitness describes her as having "a red face, a snotty nose, yellow teeth, matted hair, a moustache and boar's tusks".

She could be seeking a position at court, or maybe she just wants a husband. She thrust herself in front of the King, offering a solution to the Gromer Somer Jour problem

Gromer Somer Jour. Threatened to kill the King while out hunting because the King had given all his lands to Sir Gawain. GSJ agreed to spare His Majesty if he came back in a year with the answer to the riddle, "What do women want most in the world?"

A secret mission followed, taking the King and Sir Gawain the length and breadth of the country this past year. Their task has been to ask all the women they meet the answer to the riddle. Latest reports suggest that they now have thousands of answers but are no nearer to knowing which one will satisfy GSJ. A

woman called Ragnell, richly dressed, riding a good horse, but ugly as sin intercepted Arthur in the forest. The King reports she told him that all the answers he had so far were useless. She offered to tell him the right answer, but only if he made Sir Gawain marry her. HM returned to court, where Sir Gawain agreed to Ragnell's terms in order to save HM's life.

HM then met with Gromer Somer Jour

and gave him Ragnell's answer, which is, "What women want most in the world is power over men." Judging by the rage displayed by GSJ, this was the correct answer.

Note: The threat to the King's life has been removed, but the court is in the unhappy situation of having to accept this sinister woman as wife to Sir G – to say nothing of what Sir Gawain must feel!

DAME RAGNELL - UPDATE: SEE ENCLOSED REPORT FROM SIR GAWAIN TO HM KING ARTHUR

Sire,

I write to tell you of the amazing change in my fortunes. As you know, the day of my marriage was a sad day for all of us for, although my bride wore a dress of gorgeous silk, I could hardly bear to look upon her face.

I have to confess that when the wedding banquet was over, I mounted the stone steps to the bedchamber with a stone in my heart. How was I to perform my duty as a husband, I asked myself?

Then in my bedchamber in the flickering light of the candles, something very odd happened. When I turned to face my wife, I saw not a hideous old crone but a beautiful young woman with long hair like burnished gold!

"Who are you?" I asked her, astonished.

"I am your wife," the young woman replied. "And now you have a choice. You can have me fair by day, or fair by night, but not both.

125

You must make up your mind."

Well, my lord, I confess I did not know what to say. If I had her fair by night, I would have the embarrassment of an ugly wife by day, and pity of the whole court; but if I had her fair by day, then I would have to come upstairs to the hideous woman at night. I thought and thought, but I couldn't decide. Finally, I said the only thing I could say,

CENSORED

Sir Gawain de Mole'd'Orkney.

The answer Sir Gawain gave his wife is not available from the A-MI5 files. Can you guess what it was?

Answer: Sir Gawain told his wife the truth — that he couldn't decide. "You'll have to decide for me," he told her. At this Dame Ragnell was absolutely delighted — he had given her what women want most in the world: **power.** And because he had done that, the spell under which she had been living was broken. Now she could remain fair and beautiful *all the time.*

LEGEND 7: SIR LANCELOT'S LADY

Even though Sir Lancelot was the Queen's Knight, other women were always falling in love with him, and trying to make him break his vow to serve her. Most of the time they didn't manage it – but there was one woman who did. She had a baby boy who was to grow up to outdo his father as the best knight in the world. Read who she was, and how she did it, in legend number seven – as she gives an exclusive interview to *PRITHEE!*, the Arthurian photo mag about the rich and famous.

PRITHEE! EXCLUSIVE!
ELAINE OF CARBONEK - A VISION OF COURAGE

The daughter of the wounded Fisher King speaks of the troubles which have beset her noble family.

In her youth she was called the most beautiful woman in the world and for that, jealous Morgan le Fay cast a spell on her for five long years. Last month she left the mysterious Castle Carbonek, where she lives quietly with her father, King Pelles, the crippled Fisher King, and her young son Galahad. Accompanied by the family's ancient hermit, Naciens, she came to court with Galahad, now aged 12, where mother and son were graciously received by the King and Queen. Still a radiantly beautiful woman, despite the many difficulties which have beset her and her noble family, Elaine had brought Galahad to meet his father, Sir Lancelot, newly returned from the wars in France. But this week she returned to the ruined castle where she lives, and there for the first time ever she graciously agreed to be interviewed for *PRITHEE!* magazine.

The castle has lain in ruins for twenty years since Sir Balyn wounded King Pelles – the blow he struck that day is called the "Dolorous Blow".

The cosy chamber where the Lady Elaine sits and spins.

Galahad, 12, has the same handsome looks as his father, Sir Lancelot. Here with his mother he looks out from the ruined castle battlements over the Waste Lands.

Elaine's new hairstyle wowed everyone – except Lancelot.

You were born into one of the most distinguished families in the land – the "Grail family". Can you explain what that means?

My father is a descendant of Joseph of Arimathea, the uncle of Jesus Christ. Joseph was a tin merchant and came to do business in Cornwall – some say he brought the boy Jesus with him. In the days after Jesus was crucified by the Romans, Joseph came back to Britain, bringing with him the cup or "grail" that was used at the Last Supper.

Was that the only relic?

No. He also brought the spear which the centurion had thrust into Jesus' side.

Joseph later died at my family home, Castle Carbonek, and left the cup and the spear in the safekeeping of my ancestors.

Is it true that the same cup is still in your family's possession?

Quite true. Ever since that time the grail and the spear – known as "the Hallows" – have been kept safely in a tower at Carbonek. When a truly worthy knight comes to Carbonek, the Hallows mysteriously leave the room in which they are kept and appear before him.

Can you tell us how the castle came to be ruined? Is it true that it fell down at exactly the same time that your father received the terrible wound to his thigh?

Yes, that is quite true. It happened right at the beginning of King Arthur's reign, just after I was born. One of King Arthur's knights, a wild man called Sir Balyn, killed another knight called Garlon in the great hall of Carbonek. It was a very shocking incident, because as you know, knights are not supposed to come armed to the dinner table. My father told Sir Balyn he must die, grabbed a huge

sword that was hanging on the wall, and broke Sir Balyn's sword in bits. Sir Balyn then ran through the many stone passages of Carbonek, up winding stairs, through arches, along battlements, looking everywhere for a weapon with which to fight my father. Finally, he came to the closed door of the room in the tower where the Hallows were kept. It is said that as he pushed open the door he heard a voice warning him not to go in, but he could hear my father's footsteps behind him on the stairs, and he could see no one in the room, so in he went.

In the room was a table, covered with a pure white cloth, and on the table was the Grail, covered by another cloth. But what caught Sir Balyn's eye was the holy spear, hanging point down in the air, dripping blood as it always did. He seized it, and turned to face my father.

My father, who knew what that room contained, had dropped his weapon, and was standing defenceless in the doorway, his eyes full of love because he was in the presence of the Grail. Sir Balyn did not care. He plunged the holy spear deep into my father's thigh. When he did that, it was as if an earthquake and a whirlwind hit the castle all at once – it shook and cracked and fell in on itself, and the land for miles around was laid waste. To this day, nothing grows on these "Waste Lands" and most of the castle lies in ruins. And of course, my father's wound has never healed.

It must have been an unbelievably difficult time for you all.

Yes. We have managed to make parts of the castle weatherproof and quite comfortable. But for the Waste Lands, and my poor father, there has been no help. At least, not yet.

What happened to Sir Balyn?

Nothing good. He killed his own brother, not realizing who he was, and died himself soon after.

You have also suffered greatly – at the hands of Morgan le Fay?

Morgan did not care for the way people spoke of my beauty. She cast a spell on me which meant that I was stuck in a tub of scalding water, unable to get out, night or day for five whole years. My father

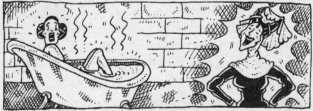

knew that the spell could only be broken by the best knight in the world, so when he heard Sir Lancelot was riding close by, he begged him to come and rescue me. You cannot imagine what a relief it was when Sir Lancelot came through the door, still in his armour, and lifted me from that scalding tub. That night, at supper – the first time I had eaten in the great hall for five years – the Hallows appeared. I did not need that to show me Sir Lancelot was a worthy knight, but all the same – it was a telling sign.

Your son Galahad was conceived that night. Was this a whirlwind romance, or is it true what people say – that you cast a spell on him to make him break his vow to the Queen?

I believe Sir Lancelot has always said he was enchanted. I have never known quite what he meant by that. He behaved as if he was in love. Of course, I am very sorry for the trouble it caused between him and the Queen, but all these things have happened for the best. Merlin always said that Galahad would be the one to heal my father's wound.

The same day that Lancelot rescued me, he killed a dragon who was living in the tomb of our ancestors. There was an inscription on that tomb. It said, "There shall come a leopard of king's blood, and he will slay this dragon." As everyone knows, Sir Lancelot has three leopards on his shield. But there was a second part of the inscription which nobody understood. It said, "This leopard will father a lion who will surpass all other knights."

You think the lion is your son Galahad?

Yes, of course. He will be a great knight, greater even than his father.

Your father clearly wants Lancelot to acknowledge the boy as his son.

Naturally. Galahad is his son. Lancelot should do no less.

Last week your father sent you to Camelot as his representative. He also sent you as Lancelot's wife. How do you feel about the fact that Lancelot did not appear at court the whole time you were there?

Lancelot must do as he sees fit. The day will come when he will be proud to acknowledge Galahad – and when that day comes, perhaps he will find it in his heart to acknowledge the feelings he had for me, too.

You are looking especially lovely with your new hairstyle. Did you braid it like that in the hope of re-awakening Lancelot's love?

Everyone likes a change now and then. I thought my hair looked a little severe pulled back from my face. This looks softer. I doubt very much whether Lancelot would have noticed.

People say it was fear of the Queen's anger which made Lancelot leave you – and which makes him keep a low profile now. Yet you don't seem bitter.

No, I'm not bitter. Lancelot took a vow when he was a very young man to serve the Queen, which he broke the night he spent with me. If he now thinks that vow is more important than being a husband to me, and a father to his son, then I have to accept it. We will all answer to God our Maker in the end.

Do you regret your fling?

For me it was not a fling. I loved Lancelot, and still love him. Of course I do not regret it. He saved me from a terrible fate, and he gave me a beautiful son, who will one day bring great glory to King Arthur's court, heal my father and restore the Waste Lands around Castle Carbonek. What is there to regret?

FANTASTIC FACTS 7: KNIGHTHOOD IN THE MIDDLE AGES

• Young Galahad was a dead cert for knighthood. He was a boy, and he came from a noble family. It didn't really matter that he had a single mum, and his dad refused to have anything to do with him.

• Any heavily armed knight needed a horse that was big and strong enough to carry him into battle. Only when men learned how to breed such horses, and invented the saddle and stirrup to keep the knight on the horse, did the medieval knight come into being.

• The word "chivalry" comes from "*chevalier*" – the French word for horseman, which also came to mean "knight". A knight was just a warrior on horseback.

• Although knights came from wealthy families – armour and weapons cost a lot of money – they were often brutes and thugs. The rules of chivalry were invented to control them. There were so many armed horsemen roaming all over Europe spoiling for a fight that in 1095, Pope Urban II ordered that all boys of good family should swear an oath before a bishop to protect widows and orphans and help the poor and oppressed.

• A small-time knight was a "vassal" to his "liege lord". This meant he paid taxes to him and fought for him, and swore to be loyal, and in return the lord was supposed to protect him if he was attacked by other people. His lord would also be a vassal but to a more powerful liege lord, and so it would go on, right up to the King.

● Medieval knights were a cross between sportsmen, soldiers and policemen. As well as fighting for fun, and against their own and their lords' enemies, they went after robbers and kidnappers.

● Knighthood was part of the feudal system. Medieval society was divided into three classes: nobles, clergy and peasants. Peasants might be free men, but they might also be "villeins" which meant they could farm strips of land, or graze their animals, or take wood from the forest for their fire in return for "tithes" to the lord – this meant they had to work a set number of days a year for him, and give him a certain amount of their farm produce – and fight in his army if needed.

Wannabe a Knight?
We tell you how......

① THE GOOD NEWS IS YOU DON'T HAVE TO GO TO SCHOOL. READING, WRITING AND 'RITHMATIC WEREN'T IMPORTANT TO KNIGHTS.

② THE BAD NEWS IS YOU GET SENT AWAY FROM HOME AGED SEVEN TO GO AND LIVE WITH YOUR DAD'S LORD.

⑤ BY FOURTEEN YOU'RE DUE FOR PROMOTION AND YOU GET TO BE A SQUIRE. NOW THE WEAPONS TRAINING GETS SERIOUS, YOU PRACTISE WEARING HEAVY ARMOUR, AND YOU TEACH THE YOUNGER BOYS HOW TO FIGHT.

⑥ THE BAD NEWS IS YOU'RE STILL A BIT OF A WAITER — BUT NOW YOU CARVE MEAT AT TABLE. YOU ALSO CLEAN AND POLISH YOUR KNIGHT'S ARMOUR AND WEAPONS, AND GO WITH HIM INTO TOURNAMENTS AND WARS.

④ THEN YOU DRESS IN CLEAN CLOTHES, AND SPEND THE WHOLE NIGHT STANDING OR KNEELING, "KEEPING VIGIL" IN CHURCH.

⑧ THE GOOD NEWS IS THAT AFTER THAT YOU GO OUT INTO THE COURTYARD, WHERE ALL THE KNIGHTS AND LADIES WATCH AS YOUR ARMOUR IS PUT ON PIECE BY PIECE.

⑩ THE NEXT DAY THERE'S A CHURCH SERVICE WHERE THE PRIEST BLESSES YOUR SWORD, AND PRAYS THAT FOR THE REST OF YOUR LIFE YOU WILL "DEFEND CHURCHES, WIDOWS, ORPHANS, AND THOSE WHO SERVE GOD AGAINST THE CRUELTY OF HERETICS AND INFIDELS"

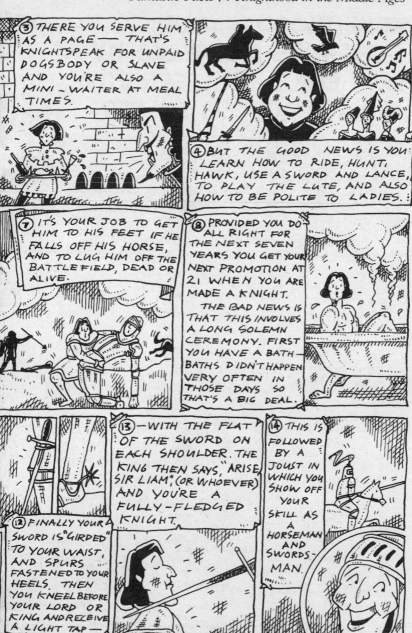

③ THERE YOU SERVE HIM AS A PAGE— THAT'S KNIGHTSPEAK FOR UNPAID DOGSBODY OR SLAVE AND YOU'RE ALSO A MINI-WAITER AT MEAL TIMES.

④ BUT THE GOOD NEWS IS YOU LEARN HOW TO RIDE, HUNT, HAWK, USE A SWORD AND LANCE, TO PLAY THE LUTE, AND ALSO HOW TO BE POLITE TO LADIES.

⑦ IT'S YOUR JOB TO GET HIM TO HIS FEET IF HE FALLS OFF HIS HORSE, AND TO LUG HIM OFF THE BATTLEFIELD, DEAD OR ALIVE.

⑧ PROVIDED YOU DO ALL RIGHT FOR THE NEXT SEVEN YEARS YOU GET YOUR NEXT PROMOTION AT 21 WHEN YOU ARE MADE A KNIGHT.
THE BAD NEWS IS THAT THIS INVOLVES A LONG SOLEMN CEREMONY. FIRST YOU HAVE A BATH— BATHS DIDN'T HAPPEN VERY OFTEN IN THOSE DAYS SO THAT'S A BIG DEAL.

⑬ —WITH THE FLAT OF THE SWORD ON EACH SHOULDER. THE KING THEN SAYS, "ARISE, SIR LIAM", (OR WHOEVER) AND YOU'RE A FULLY-FLEDGED KNIGHT.

⑭ THIS IS FOLLOWED BY A JOUST IN WHICH YOU SHOW OFF YOUR SKILL AS A HORSEMAN AND SWORDSMAN.

⑫ FINALLY YOUR SWORD IS "GIRDED" TO YOUR WAIST, AND SPURS FASTENED TO YOUR HEELS. THEN YOU KNEEL BEFORE YOUR LORD OR KING AND RECEIVE A LIGHT TAP—

KNIGHTHOOD - YOUR QUESTIONS ANSWERED BY LADY EMILY - THE SENSITIVE, CARING PROBLEM SOLVER

Dear Lady Emily,
I would like to be a knight, but I am a girl, and my olds say it is unseemly for me to fight. I don't think it's fair. Is there some sort of court that I can appeal to about this?
Anne, aged 12, Salisbury

Sorry, Anne, there's no Equal Opportunities Commission in medieval England. You should concentrate on your hawking – it's good fun and, as you know, almost every lady has her own hawk. You should also learn the gentle arts – playing the lute, singing, sewing and listening quietly and gracefully to stories.

In time you will grow up and be really glad that you don't have to lumber around in heavy armour. There is no greater thrill than having a knight mad with love for you, and wearing your favours in war. Just you leave fighting to the fellas, dear!

Dear Lady Emily,
I'm a good fighter, and I love seeing the knights in armour, and their ladies in fine clothes. I want to be a knight and

fight for a lady, but my father reckons it's not for the likes of me as we are peasants. I say he's wrong. There should be scholarships for people like me, or else I should be able to work my way up through the ranks. What do you think? Alan aged 9, Worcester

Your father is right. You'll get into a lot of trouble unless you learn to know your place. The best a boy like you can hope for is to work the land like your dad, or maybe become a stable boy. You might even be able to get work as a scullion (or drudge) in the kitchen. Don't think this is a soft option – the hours are long and it's hard and hot work, as you'll be turning whole animals on a spit over a fire.

As for fighting – it's fine for you to fight people of your own rank with a stave, but on no account should you get ideas above your station. You could also learn to use a bow and arrow, then one day you can fight for your lord as a foot soldier. But, sorry dear, Knighthood is not for the likes of you.

Dear Lady Emily,
My older brother says that when my dad dies he will get the castle, and I will get nothing. It's not fair. Why can't the land be divided equally between us?

William Fitzsimmons.

What do you think would happen if every time a noble died, his land was divided up between all his sons? Each generation would get a smaller and smaller share, until there was no land left.

Think about it. Would you want the estate divided if you were the older brother? You'll just have to get on your horse and look for adventures, like any other younger brother. There's a very good living to be made if you really try. Every time you defeat another knight in combat you get to keep his horse, armour and weapons, which you can always sell on if you don't need them yourself. Stop feeling sorry for yourself and sharpen up your fighting skills.

LEGEND 8: THE QUEST FOR THE HOLY GRAIL

In Arthurian legend, the Holy Grail was a magical chalice or cup which could only be seen by people who led very good lives. The chalice would appear without warning, always covered with white silk, surrounded by a bright light and accompanied by the most wonderful perfume. It always brought each person the food and drink he or she most desired, and just being close to it made people feel peaceful and happy.

When Galahad grew up, he was knighted by his father, Sir Lancelot, and took his place at the Round Table. Galahad's seat was the Siège Perilous, which had remained empty since the beginning of the Round Table. That night the Hallows appeared in the Great Hall at Camelot, shrouded in silk, and bathed in light. This annoyed Sir Gawain, who said that he wanted to see the Grail without its silk cover. So he started the Quest by saying that he would not return to court till he had done so. Next morning, the King and Queen watched as one hundred and fifty knights rode out of Camelot on the Quest for the Holy Grail.

What Sir Gawain did not realize was that this was an adventure like no other. This was not about conquering outer enemies, but inner ones – the things within the knights themselves that held them back from greatness: their pride and envy, fear, jealousy, anger, greed and laziness. Most of the knights did not understand that. Here in legend number eight, is what happened to three of them – Sir Gawain, Sir Lancelot and Sir Bors – when they set off in search of the Holy Grail – and then what happened when finally a very few of the very best knights achieved the Holy Grail.

THE GREATEST QUEST OF THEM ALL – SIR GAWAIN

Sir Gawain was not a bad man. He was a good fighter, brave, strong and kind. But he had many faults, including pride, a hot-temper and jealousy. It was these faults that stood between him and the sight of the Holy Grail.

Gawain was especially jealous of Sir Galahad, because Galahad was already being called the Best Knight in the World – even though he was still only a young man. Gawain decided he was definitely not going questing with Galahad, and set off in the opposite direction to look for adventures.

Day after day he rode through the land, but there were no adventures to be found. Nothing happened. He met no one. It was really boring, and the worst thing of all was, when he stopped at an abbey, the monks told him about the many brave deeds Sir Galahad was doing. Sir Gawain began to think it might be a good idea to join up with Galahad after all.

"It wouldn't change anything even if you did," one of the monks told him. "You wouldn't be happy in each other's company for long, because you are angry and jealous, and Sir Galahad is not."

Of course, this just made Gawain angrier than ever. Next morning he set off again, this time in the company of his cousin, Sir Owaine, son of Morgan le Fay, who was having a boring time as well.

The two of them had not ridden far when they came to a castle guarded by seven knights. Because they were so bored, they picked a fight with them, and finished up killing all seven. That night Sir Gawain stopped at a lonely hermitage.

"I am Sir Gawain, knight of King Arthur, and I am on a Quest for the Holy Grail," he announced importantly.

"I would rather know how things stand between you and God," answered the hermit drily.

But Sir Gawain wasn't interested in God. Instead he boasted to the hermit about all the fights he had won – including the killing of the seven knights that day. The hermit was not impressed.

"Sir Galahad unhorsed those seven single-handedly," he told Gawain. "But he didn't kill them. He had no reason to kill, and neither did you. You must do penance for this wicked deed."

"Get lost," said Gawain. "Life is difficult enough for us knights without having to do penance."

After that things went from bad to worse for Gawain. Between Pentecost and Michaelmas he didn't have a single adventure – and he wasn't the only one. Some twenty other knights wandered the land, puzzled that there were no robbers for them to chase, or wicked knights for them to challenge. They did not understand that the reason they were not having these adventures any more was because such things were easy for them; what was much more difficult was to overcome the faults within themselves.

Finally, Gawain found a fight – and then to his horror found that the knight he had killed was none other than his cousin Owaine. He was so sickened by what he had done that he returned to Camelot, wretched and unsuccessful.

SIR LANCELOT

Things went a little better for Sir Lancelot, but not much. He had seen the Holy Grail at Castle Carbonek, the night after he had rescued fair Elaine from her scalding tub, and so he decided to try and find his way back there again. He came to the Waste Lands, which lay all around the castle. They were as bare and desolate as ever, but no matter how hard he

looked for it, the castle itself seemed to have disappeared.

One night, tired after a long day in the saddle, he came to a ruined chapel. There seemed to be light inside, so he knocked at the door. No one answered. Lancelot tried the door, and found it bolted, so he climbed the ivy growing on the wall, and peered in through a broken window.

Inside was an altar covered with silk, with burning candles that filled the chapel with a soft, golden glow. It looked so calm and welcoming that Lancelot longed to go inside, but there was no way in. Wearily he went back to his horse, unsaddled it, took off his sword and helmet, and lay down on the ground to sleep.

As he lay there half-asleep, he saw two white horses pulling a stretcher, on which lay a sick knight. The sick knight was groaning and muttering to himself. "Oh, sweet Lord! How much longer must I bear this pain?"

Then the chapel door opened, and there stood Naciens, the old hermit of Carbonek who had brought Galahad to Camelot. He was holding a silver candlestick in which burned five white candles. He brought the candlestick outside, and set it on a marble slab near to where Lancelot lay asleep. Then the hermit knelt in prayer.

Now, in his dream, Lancelot saw the Holy Grail. It was covered with a spotless, snow-white cloth and it came sliding down a moonbeam to rest near the candles. The light of the Grail was so bright that the light from the candles, and the light from the moon in the sky seemed like nothing. The sick knight crawled from the stretcher, and with great difficulty stretched out his hands to touch the Grail. Lancelot thought the sick knight's hands would never reach, but he struggled and struggled. Finally his fingers touched it – and in that same moment he was cured.

Now the Grail floated up from the marble altar, moved silently across the moonlit glade, and was gone. The healed knight clambered to his feet, and bowed to Naciens the hermit.

"Thanks be to God who has cured me through the Holy Grail," he said. Then he pointed at Lancelot. "But who is this knight?" he asked Naciens. "He did not even wake when the Grail came close to him!"

"This is Lancelot of the Lake," said Naciens. "His sins weigh him down. That's why he didn't wake."

"They must be heavy sins," said the knight. "I thought he was supposed to be looking for the Grail."

Naciens nodded. He picked up Lancelot's helmet and sword, and gave them to the healed knight. Then he helped him mount Lancelot's horse and the healed knight rode away into the forest. Naciens took the silver candlestick with its candles still burning and disappeared into the ruined chapel again, closing the door after him.

Lancelot lay there unable to move, not sure whether he was awake or asleep. In a little while, however, as the moon rose high in the sky, he woke, certain he had dreamed the whole thing. Then to his horror he realized that his horse was gone ... and his helmet and his sword ... Everything he thought he had dreamed had really happened.

"Oh no!" he groaned to himself. "To lie asleep when the Grail appeared! How could I? When it came to the old-style adventures, nothing was too difficult, but this is a holy thing, and the great sin of my love for the Queen stands between me and success."

Naciens had heard him. He opened the door.

"Come in," he said. "I will help you overcome your difficulties." So Lancelot went into the ruined chapel and spent many weeks with Naciens – but he never saw the Grail again.

SIR BORS

Of all the hundred and fifty knights who rode out to find the Holy Grail, only three succeeded in their Quest: Sir Bors, Sir Percival and Sir Galahad, and they did so only after all sorts of fearsome tests. Of the three, Sir Bors was the only one who returned to Camelot to tell the tale.

Sir Bors was a young knight, and good man. He knew that so long as he had nothing on his conscience he would be able to find the Grail. So the first thing he did when he started on the Grail Quest was to confess his sins to a priest. He swore a solemn oath that he would love no woman until he had achieved the Holy Grail. Only then did he set off – and then his tests began.

As he rode through the forest he came upon two knights who had tied a third knight naked to a horse, and were beating him with thorny branches. To his horror, Bors saw it was his brother, Lionel. He rushed to rescue his brother – but before he could do anything, he heard a woman screaming for help. Sir Bors turned and saw a man dragging her off into the bushes. Now he didn't know what to do. He couldn't bear to turn his back on his brother, but as a knight, he was sworn to help women and children in need. So he asked the Lord Jesus Christ to look after his brother, and rode into the bushes to rescue the lady.

It didn't take him long to see off her attacker – but he was too late to save his brother. When he came back to the path, Lionel lay dead, and there was no sign of the men who had been attacking him. Blaming himself, and full of grief, Sir Bors laid the body across his saddle, and took him to a ruined chapel. There he laid him on a marble slab to await burial.

Before he could bury him, a priest came by who told Bors he was near a castle where a lady lived who had been in love with him for a long time. She had sworn to die if Sir Bors did not return her love. If he did return it, then he would bring about the death of his uncle, Sir Lancelot. Sir Bors was horrified. He loved and admired his Uncle Lancelot more than anyone else in the world.

Sir Bors thought he would stay away from the castle, but somehow he came upon it anyway and saw a high tower full of knights and ladies, dancing, laughing and feasting. As if he was enchanted, he went inside. He was made welcome and given a beautiful cloak lined with ermine to keep him warm. The horror of his brother's death simply faded from his mind as if it had never happened. Then, through all the happy, feasting people, a lady came towards him who was more beautiful than any Sir Bors had ever seen.

"I am the Lady of the Castle, and I love you, Bors," she said.

As he heard her words, and felt himself drawn by her beauty, Sir Bors became uneasy. The memory of his dead brother came back to him. There was something else as well – some warning a hermit had given him about Sir Lancelot. But above all, there was the vow he had taken before he set out on the Quest.

"Lady, I cannot love you," he whispered. "I am sorry, for you are very lovely. But I have sworn never to love any woman until I have succeeded in my Quest for the Holy Grail."

This only made the lady more insistent.

"If you refuse me I will throw myself to my death from

151

the top of the tower," she told him. "More, I will make twelve of my gentlewomen jump with me. Surely the gallant Sir Bors does not want to be responsible for such a tragedy?"

It seemed she meant it, for she then led her ladies up the stone steps that curved up the side of the tower. From the battlements, one of the ladies called down to Sir Bors to save her.

"All you have to do is love my lady," she shouted. "Please, gallant knight – is that such a hardship?"

Sir Bors closed his eyes and prayed. He knew it must be wrong to break his vow. He also knew that he was not responsible for what other people chose to do. All the same, it was very hard – especially when he opened his eyes and saw the ladies jumping to their deaths, one after another. He made the sign of the cross on himself. As he did so, he heard the most terrifying yells around him. It was as if all the fiends of hell had been let loose – but in that moment, the tower, the lady, her gentlewomen all disappeared into thin air, and Bors was back at the chapel where his brother lay, and then that too vanished along with what he thought was his brother's body.

He was alone and safe. Had it all been a dream? Giving thanks to God that he had found the strength to stick to his duty, he continued on his Quest.

THE ACHIEVEMENT OF THE GRAIL

After many more adventures and trials, Sir Bors met up again with Sir Percival and Sir Galahad, and the three good knights came once more to Castle Carbonek. King Pelles still lay on his bed of pain, his wound unhealed. He gave a feast to celebrate their arrival, but the three knights were fasting. All they ate was bread and water.

It was during the feast that the doors of the Great Hall suddenly swung open, and in came three ghostly damsels, carrying the bleeding spear, a silver dish and a candlestick. Behind them came the Grail Maiden, carrying the Grail itself, covered by a white silk cloth.

The procession moved up the hall. As it drew near to Sir Galahad, he shouted out for it to stop. He drew his sword, and held it by the blade, so that the hilt stood high above his head like a cross, with its jewels catching the light. As if he was in a trance, he left his place at the table and took his place at the head of the procession. Through the length of the Great Hall he went, then out, and through the cold passages beyond. Naciens, the old hermit of Carbonek, told Percival and Bors to carry King Pelles in his couch, and follow. Naciens himself brought up the rear.

There was no need for candles, for the light that shone from the Grail lit up the dark passages of Castle Carbonek. At last they came to the chapel. The candlestick and the silver dish were placed on the altar, while the bleeding spear hung in the air. Percival and Bors laid King Pelles on the steps of the altar, and knelt beside him.

Then the Grail Maiden offered the Grail to Naciens.

"I have been holy priest to the Grail for many a year now," he said. "For I was young in the days of Joseph of Arimathea. I did him great wrong. So, in penance, it has been my destiny to live for all these hundreds of years, the guardian of the Grail until the day Sir Galahad should come. Now he is here, I can depart in peace."

With that Naciens offered the Grail to Sir Galahad. Galahad knelt, took the Grail, and drank from it. As he did, a great sense of peace came over him, and his whole being glowed with light and happiness. He took the weary old man, Naciens, in his arms, and kissed his head. Naciens sighed with contentment and his soul slipped quietly from his body.

Next, Sir Galahad reached his hand out for the bleeding spear, and turned to the wounded King Pelles. He held it so the drops of blood that fell from it fell on to the poor King's wound. At the instant the blood touched the wound, the King was cured.

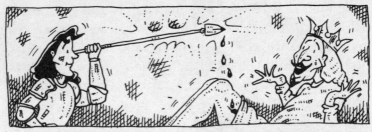

Now Sir Galahad invited Sir Bors and Sir Percival to drink from the Grail. It was his last action for his earthly duty was done. He had achieved the Holy Grail, drunk from it, and helped to heal the maimed King. There was nothing more for him to do on Earth, and so, in utter happiness, brimming with glory, his soul flew from his body and merged with the light of God.

And all the while the Grail was leaving mankind too, travelling on a sunbeam up into the heavens, never to be seen again on Earth. Why was this? Men had taken it for granted. They had put their own selfish ambition before spiritual things. They hadn't honoured it, so now it was withdrawn. That also meant that the days of Arthur's kingdom, Logres, the land of chivalry, were numbered.

Sir Percival became a monk, but he too lived for only a short time. Only Sir Bors returned to Camelot to tell his fellow knights about the wonders of the Holy Grail. For the rest of his life he lived like an ordinary knight – but he never ever forgot the great experiences he had had in the presence of the Holy Grail.

FANTASTIC FACTS 8: QUESTIONS ABOUT THE QUEST

1 What is a quest?

To quest for something means to seek or pursue something very important to you. The knights of medieval Europe were always going off questing – usually this just meant looking for adventure, which meant looking for a good fight.

However, Sir Palomides, a Saracen (Muslim) knight, spent his life questing for the Questing Beast. This was a weird creature. It had the head of a snake, the body of a leopard and the feet of a deer. It was pure white, with eyes green like emeralds, and from inside its belly came the noise of baying hounds. The Questing Beast spent its life trying to escape the sound of these hounds. No one knew why or what it was, and Sir Palomides swore he would find out. This didn't stop him having lots of other adventures, defending ladies, and cutting off the heads of their enemies.

2 Why is the first part of the word question underlined above?

Because the words "quest" and "question" are related – they come from the same "root". A question is asking for an answer, usually in words. On a quest, people are usually looking for a thing – an animal or hidden treasure – or an experience, like an adventure, or trying to find the Holy Grail.

3 Did the real King Arthur's real knights really go off questing for the Holy Grail?

Probably not. They were more interested in Druid priests and magic scabbards than Christian relics. If Arthur's warlords were after something, it was probably a Magic Cauldron.

4 So why were the knights looking for a cauldron? Didn't they have enough?

This one would have been special – a bit like the Round Table. Maybe Arthur needed the magic cauldron to prove he had the blessings of the Otherworld to stay in power.

Or maybe the other knights wanted to find the cauldron because that would mean one of them could be king. When the cauldron disappeared at the end of the story, it meant Arthur didn't have the Otherworld's blessings any more and the Kingdom of Logres was doomed.

5 There's none of that in the story you told.

No, because the Christian story has become the famous one – but there are things which are a bit odd for a Christian story. The Grail is carried by a woman – that would never have happened in medieval Europe. It could have happened in Celtic Britain, especially if the dish in question was something to do with a king-making ritual.

6 So what happened to Merlin and Morgan le Fay then? If it's a Celtic story why aren't they in it?

The medieval storytellers turned it into a story which had meaning for them – a Christian story. The Druid priests and priestesses disappeared to be replaced by Christian monks and hermits.

7 What's the difference between a monk and a hermit?

Monks belonged to monastic orders. They lived in monasteries, lots of them together. They farmed the land, copied manuscripts by hand in the days before there was any printing, prayed six or seven times a day, and sometimes kept their monasteries open as hostels for travellers.

Hermits were loners. They lived in remote places, often in caves or ruined chapels, spending their lives in prayer. From the stories it seems that they also gave overnight shelter to travelling knights and others.

8 The hermit told Sir Gawain he would have to do penance. What does that mean?

Doing penance means doing something difficult or painful to show you are sorry for your sins. Often it was walking barefoot over long distances. Much later in the story, Sir Lancelot offered to walk barefoot in penance for killing Sir Gawain's brothers, but Sir Gawain wasn't having it.

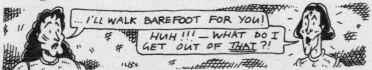

9 Who was Sir Percival?

Sir Percival is one of the Grail Knights. Here's his story: Young Perce was brought up by his widowed mother, deep in the forest, so he had none of the usual knightly training.

He wore animal skins and hunted using darts. When he was 15, some knights from King Arthur's court rode into the forest, and because he had never seen anyone except his mother till then, he thought they were angels. Sir Lancelot put him right, and told him to go to Arthur's court at Caerleon. His mother was sad to see him go.

On his first night away from home, he came to a mysterious pavilion where he found a lady asleep. He fell in love with her, and swapped rings with her while she slept. When he arrived at court, Sir Kay, who was King Arthur's seneschal (seni-shall) – that meant he was in charge of running the royal household – was very rude to him and called him a goatherd. That same day a knight in red armour swaggered into the Great Hall and snatched King Arthur's gold cup from him. King Arthur said it was not worth wasting a knight on the Red Knight, and that a squire should go after him, so Percival volunteered. He caught up with the knight, and killed him with one of his hunting darts. Now the Red Knight's armour and horse belonged to him. The trouble was Perce didn't know how to get the knight out of his armour! He thought he would set fire to the body to get rid of it when another knight called Gonemans arrived and showed him how the armour came off piece by piece.

Gonemans took him home with him and taught him all the things a knight needed to know. Perce then rode out in search of adventures – and also to look for the mysterious lady whose ring he wore – before returning to King Arthur's court to take his place in the seat next to the Siege Perilous.

10 Is there any truth in the legend that Joseph of Arimathea brought the cup used by Jesus at the Last Supper to Britain?

Who knows? It's possible, but on balance, the Holy Grail seems most likely to have been a vision. The story of the Quest of the Holy Grail shows the path of knighthood had become a way to know God.

ARE YOU SEEING THINGS AGAIN?

LEGEND 9: LANCELOT'S OTHER LADY

Sir Lancelot seems to have had a thing about ladies called Elaine. Years after the mother of Sir Galahad, Elaine of Carbonek had died, Lancelot met Elaine of Astolat and wore her colours in a tournament. Now, coming in at number 9 in the Ten Best Arthurian Legends Ever is the story of that tournament as told on live television by sports commentators Des Lance-up and Bob Buckler, and newscaster Emilia Lotsamagica.

OLD PLAYER, NEW STRIP

Des Lance-up: Good afternoon and welcome to the great Lists of Camelot once again. This is Des Lance-up in the press box looking down on this long, green field on this beautiful June day. The pennants are flying, the stands are full of ladies in their finery, the weather's kind so far – a light wind, and not too hot, for which I'm sure our armoured heroes will be grateful. As you've probably heard, there's everything to play for here today because champion Lancelot du Lac, who's swept the board for the past eight years and taken home the diamond every time, has this year stepped down from the competition to make way for a younger man. Over to you, Bob!

Bob Buckler: Thanks, Des. Yes, they're riding into the field now, these gallant knights. What a sight! The finest British jousters, mounted on their sturdy steeds. The horses and riders, of course, are clothed in matching colours, reds,  blues, greens, embroidered with gold and silver. As they come in at the trot a great roar goes up from the crowd in the stands, and you can probably hear the words of "Flower of Scotland" rising like a great cry of triumph from the visiting supporters. Yes, it's the visiting team, led by the King of Scots and the Knights of Northumberland that is parading past the royal box now. Their Majesties, King Arthur and Queen Guinevere, are waving graciously. One wonders what's going through the Queen's mind, because this is the first year in living memory when her champion has not been leading the field. That may mean that the diamond is not brought back to Camelot this evening. But if Guinevere is feeling anything, it's not showing – Her Majesty is as serene and dignified as always. But now into the arena come the home side – visors up, of course, at this stage. Oh, there's a great wave of sound as the home supporters sing "Camelot Forever, Forever Camelot" and I can see Sir Kay, there, and beside him, Sir Brandiles. There's Sir Sagramor, Sir Dodinas and Sir Lucan. They're riding up to the far end of the field. The visitors have won the toss, so they have the sun behind them for the first tourney. As they line up their mounts at the starting line, I can see the marshal with his pennant held high, ready for the off. The bugles sound and they're holding their lances at the ready. The herald brings his arm down and they're off!

Des Lance-up: What a sight that is, Bob, as two groups of thirty warhorses thunder up the field, hooves throwing up huge bits of turf. Now there's the crash and clatter as they connect – what a noise as sixty lances thump on to shields and helmets and breastplates.

Oh, and there are seven, eight, nine – nine northerners down at that first strike! It looks from here as if at least three of those aren't going to be getting up again. It's hard to tell what's happening now, as the riders wheel and make short charges again. Oh, and now it's Sir Sagramor who's taken a tumble, and oh, his horse has fallen! His horse has fallen and rolled on top of him! The herald has blown his bugle, the marshals are carrying Sir Sagramor from the field. The horse is also led away. It's amazing the amount of damage these knights can do even with the tips of their lances encased in wood.

Bob Buckler: Not surprising really, I suppose, because they get up to speeds of some ten miles an hour.

Des Lance-up: Absolutely! If you think of two horsemen approaching each other at that speed, each with a six foot oak pole, that pole held steady is quite capable of splitting a man's head and ribs and goodness knows what else.

Bob Buckler: Now they're regrouping for the second charge, and despite the loss of Sir Sagramor, it's still looking good for the King's side. They've only lost one man, the visitors are down nine, no ten, because it looks as if Sir Simon Newcastle has retired with a broken arm. But wait a minute – something very interesting looks to be happening now. There's a new knight! A new knight has joined the away side. I don't know who this knight can be! Do you, Desmond?

Des Lance-up: Well, he certainly doesn't want us to know. He's dressed in black armour, he's got no markings on his shield, no markings at all.

Bob Buckler: He's a big man, and he's wearing what looks like a red favour on his helmet, I can't see what it is from this distance – his visor's down, of course, so no one can see his face. This man definitely does not want to be recognized.

Des Lance-up: No, and it's obvious the away team weren't expecting this, because there seems to be some dispute about where he's going to fit in the formation. But the herald's telling them all to get on with it – and they're off! They're off  again. Oh, can this man fight! He's sent five men flying, they're down like dominoes, and that's not all. He's not pausing for a second, there's another one, and another – this man is a fighting whirlwind. It's a pity Lancelot isn't here today to give him a run for his money. But oh! oh! His horse is down! And Sir Bors – it looks as if he's got half of Sir Bors' spear in his side. He has. The Dark Knight has half a spear in his side! Well, it looks as if that's him finished for today.

Bob Buckler: No! The young knight who was with him, he's wearing the colours of Astolat, I think he must be Bernard of Astolat's younger son, and he's knocked off one of his own team, he's knocked the King of Scots off his horse. Now he's grabbing the horse, and forcing his way into the contest, and swiping them right, left and centre, swiping them all aside, he's giving the Dark Knight a second chance.

Des Lance-up: The Dark Knight is taking it, spear in his side or not. The spear's still sticking out of him but he's hauled himself up on that horse, and he's laying about him with his sword – that's Sir Bors down now for Camelot, Sir Bors and Sir Ector. They're trying to make a comeback, but the Dark Knight's not having any of it, he's knocked their helmets off – and they're out of the fight. But he's not resting on his laurels, he's dishing out the same treatment to everyone who attacks him. This is incredible jousting prowess we're seeing here today! This mysterious knight is an amazing fighter! They're lying in heaps around him – there's no question now that King Arthur's Knights of the Round Table have lost the fight today.

Bob Buckler: Yes, Des, they have. There's the bugle now. That's the final bugle, the call to lodging. The Round Table have lost and the diamond will undoubtedly be going to the Dark Knight. As he passes beneath our box on the way to lodging, I can  see that the favour he's wearing is a red sleeve, a red sleeve embroidered with pearls. I wonder which of the ladies present here today gave him that?

Des Lance-up: A lady who's going to be very happy tonight, I'd say, when he presents her with the ninth diamond. Join us later, after the presentation, when we go down to the lodging and try to interview this extraordinary knight.

Later the same day...

Des Lance-up: Well, as you know I had hoped to bring you a live interview with the Dark Knight. But instead I have to tell you that the Dark Knight is not to be found. He disappeared as mysteriously as he arrived. He did not  go up to the Queen to receive the diamond, and at first people thought this might be because he was receiving medical attention for his wound. But none of the surgeons here have seen him, no one's bound his wounds, and he's vanished without trace. I have here with me Master Simon Postlethwaite, apothecary of this town. Tell me, Master, you saw that lance embedded in the Dark Knight's side. What sort of wound would you say that would cause?

Simon Postlethwaite: Undoubtedly broken ribs, Master Desmond. Then depending how deep the point had penetrated, there could be damage to internal organs...

Des Lance-up: So it could be a mortal wound?

Simon Postlethwaite: Indeed, sir.

Des Lance-up: He didn't look – so far as I could see – to be bleeding too severely.

Simon Postlethwaite: That can only have been because the spear was staunching the flow.

Des Lance-up: So if someone tried to extract the spear, that's when the trouble could really start?

Simon Postlethwaite: Absolutely. The man needs a skilful surgeon.

Des Lance-up: Thank you. So, you heard what Master Postlethwaite said. If anyone's sheltering the Dark Knight, for whatever reason, we appeal to you to come forward, so that this hero can get the medical attention he needs. I gather Sir Gawain's been organizing a search in case he's fainted somewhere from loss of blood. In the meantime, who he is, and where he came from remains a mystery. We'll bring you any fresh developments in our next bulletin.

A week later...

Des Lance-up: Well, this is Des Lance-up for Celtic Television once more with the news that the mystery knight who dominated the tournament at Camelot last week has been identified. I'm told that when Sir Bors stayed at the castle of

Astolat on his way back to London, he learned that the Dark Knight had stayed there and left behind his shield. Sir Bors asked to see it and when it was shown to him, he recognized it immediately by the three golden leopards on a blue background. I don't suppose there's anyone alive in the realm today who doesn't know that those are the colours of none other than – **Sir Lancelot du Lac.**

Of course, that explains the extraordinary fighting skill of this knight. The fact that he was wearing a favour – not the Queen's – may also explain why he was so shy to claim his prize. But this can only be speculation at this stage. What is certain is that although his identity has been established, his current whereabouts remain a mystery. He did not return to Astolat, and fears are mounting that he may have crawled away to die.

Three weeks later...

Des Lance-up: As you know, it's more than a month since the tournament at Camelot, and during all that time, we've not known whether Sir Lancelot du Lac is alive or dead. Well, the news today is that he's very much alive, and

that he will be returning to the court soon! It seems he's been nursed back to health by Sir Lavaine, the younger son of Sir Bernard of Astolat, and what is likely to cause a lot more excitement among the press, by Sir Bernard's lovely daughter, Elaine, a young maiden of great beauty whom they've already christened the Lily Maid of Astolat. So one can't help but wonder if that red favour that Lancelot was wearing the day he carried everything before him at Camelot had been given to him by the Fair Maid. If so, it remains to be seen what sort of welcome he receives from the Queen when she presents him with his ninth diamond...

A *week* after that ...

Des Lance-up:
Welcome to Westminster, where we bring you live coverage of Sir Lancelot du Lac's return to Camelot. I'm here in the Great Hall, and Sir Lancelot has just come in – and I have to say that he is receiving a hero's welcome. He's  walking through the assembled knights and their ladies, and the cheers – well, you can hear – they're raising the roof as now he approaches the King and Queen, and bows. If the Queen feels any jealousy that he entered that tourney wearing another woman's favour, it certainly isn't showing now as she presents him with the diamond. Perhaps the fact he came so close to death has made her glad to see him anyway. She's smiling, she's

giving him the diamond – the ninth diamond, he also has the diamonds from all the eight previous contests, and now he's turning to acknowledge the cheers of the crowd. This man is unbelievable. He's twice the age of many of the youngsters in the lists, but there's still no one in the whole of Logres who can touch him...

But what's happening now? There's some sort of kerfuffle. I think maybe a messenger has arrived – certainly people are moving out of the hall, they seem to be moving down towards the river ... We'll bring you more news when we know what's happening...

Later that evening ...

Emilia Lotsamagica: Good evening. This is Emilia Lotsamagica with News at Ten from Celtic Television. Today at Westminster, Sir Lancelot du Lac received the ninth diamond from Her Majesty the Queen – but the ceremony was brought to an abrupt end when a strange barge, draped in black, glided down river, and moored at the palace steps. Our reporter, Des Lance-up, was at the scene. What can you tell us, Des?

Des Lance-up: Well, it was a beautiful afternoon here, Emilia, and as you said, the barge arrived in the middle of the ceremony. It was rowed by an old, dumb oarsman, and there was a single figure lying in it, dressed in white.

The oarsman brought it to the palace steps, and there he shipped his oars. One by one, the knights of the court came down to the steps where the barge lay rocking; Sir Lancelot was among them. By this time it was clear that the figure in the barge was Elaine of Astolat – the Lily Maid – and that she was dead. She was lying in state, and apparently she had a letter in her hand. The King arrived, and was handed the letter. I'm told he read it, and that he passed it to Sir Lancelot. From what I can gather, the young damsel died of love. It seems she'd fallen head over heels for Sir Lancelot, and that he was unable to return her affection. I understand there's no suggestion of any real romance between them – this is a case of a young woman falling in love with a man old enough to be her father, and, in fact, he behaved like a true knight, very responsibly. But the girl is dead of a broken heart and, of course, although everyone's putting a brave face on it, this can only be seen as one more blow – at a very difficult time – to the unity of the Round Table. This is Des Lance-up, for Celtic Television, at the royal palace of Camelot …

FANTASTIC FACTS 9: JOUSTS AND TOURNAMENTS

1 Tournaments were the great sporting events of medieval times. They were a way of giving knights practice as fighters. They also stopped them from getting bored when there were no wars to fight. As described by the Arthurian storytellers, tournaments were held on long fields called "lists" that were lined by brightly-coloured pavilions, or tents, where the spectators stood or, if they were very posh, sat to watch – just like the stands for sports spectators today. Inside the stands were rails to stop idiots from wandering out into the path of the horses – and the horses from running into the stands. A tournament was a good day out for the family and, just like sporting fixtures today, tournaments attracted big crowds, and with them, pedlars and pickpockets. There would also be an ale tent for refreshments.

2 Every tournament had a **Queen of the Joust**. She was the dishiest dame (or the highest ranking lady present) and it was her job to give the prize to the bravest knight – or at least to the one left standing at the end. Women were also involved by giving their "favours". Each knight would wear his lady's favour – a scarf, a glove, a lock of hair or, as in this story, a sleeve (what happened to her dress, did she wear it with only one arm?) – fastened to his helmet or sleeve. The phrase "to wear your heart on your sleeve" dates from this time.

3 A **Knight Errant** was a wandering knight. "Errant" is an old French word meaning "wandering in search of adventure". The reason such a knight wandered was very simple. He had no land – he was a younger son, and all a father's lands usually went to the oldest brother. A Knight Errant made his living by tilting at jousts – he was a bit like a professional sportsman today. If he won against a rich knight, he could take him prisoner and demand a ransom. At the very least he would get to keep the horse and armour of his defeated foe.

4 The referee at a tournament was called the **Herald**. This was because as well as knowing the Rules of the Lists he could also interpret the markings on the shields of the knights – their coats-of-arms – and know exactly who they were and what family they came from, even when he couldn't see their faces because they were encased from head to toe in armour. As the knights rode into the lists he would announce their names and give a big spiel about all the victories they had won in the past.

5 Jousting was a high-risk sport, and every knight kitted themselves out accordingly. There was so much protective clothing, and it was extremely difficult to put on and move in it, that his squire had to help him with every piece. The first layer was a quilted vest with a hood attached – this was mainly to stop the armour from digging in and causing nasty sores in tender places. Next came the chain-mail jerkin, helmet and leggings. These looked as if they had been knitted out of steel thread. Next the knight was strapped into a heavy breastplate, shin guards and elbow guards. Over the top of this went a tunic with the knight's coat-of-arms on it – this would help him to be recognized and also stop his armour from rusting (there was no stainless steel in those days). Finally, his squire put a helmet over the knight's head. This looked like an upturned bucket with a small slit to see out of and a few holes through which to breathe. It was pretty hard to bend by this time, so his squire strapped sharp spurs to his heels. Now all the squire had to do was get the poor, half-blind knight up on to his horse, and then hand him his lance, or spear, his sword and his shield.

6 If you're starting to feel sorry for the knight, spare a thought for his poor horse who didn't even choose to go into combat. Like his master, the horse wore padding, and chain-mail, and then a top-covering, colour co-ordinated with his master's coat-of-arms. On top of all this was placed an enormous saddle. Saddles had increasingly high pommels back and front, in order to stop the top-heavy, armoured rider from falling off. Like master, like horse – all this protection made it hard to move and harder still to see anything other than what was straight ahead.

7 We use the word tournament or joust interchangeably, but in fact they were two different events. A tournament, or tourney, which is what Lancelot got into when he wore the favour of the Lily Maid of Astolat, was a team event. Two groups of knights charged each other with blunted lances, and fought till one side won. It was like a battle, rough and muddled, and lots of knights got badly hurt. A joust was when two knights challenged each other to single combat. Spectators preferred jousts, because they could see the skill of the fighters more easily. The expression "to go full tilt at something" dates from this time.

8 In jousting there was scoring – a point was scored for hitting an opponent's helmet, for example. Each knight was allowed to break three lances before he was out of the contest. If both men smashed their lances, they dismounted and continued the fight on foot with swords. If you knocked someone's helmet off, it meant you could cut off his head. So it really wasn't his day – or, er, (k)night!

9 If you fell down during a tourney or a joust the only person allowed to help you to get up was your own squire. Squires watched from the sidelines, cheering on their lords, and waiting like ball-boys to see if they had to run into the fray to haul their lord to his feet.

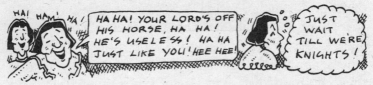

10 In fact, the tournaments we read about in Arthurian legend are a romantic version. The earliest tournaments had no pennants or pretty ladies watching from the stands. They were money-making events. A local lord would announce he was holding a tournament, and the battleground would be the road between two towns. Some pens made of wicker would be made up nearby – these were the original "lists" – where tired knights could rest till they got their breath back. Then, on the day, knights armed with real weapons rode up from opposite directions, and everyone coming from one direction fought everyone coming from the other.

The wicker pens, or lists, were neutral ground. If you were stunned or winded, you could take shelter there till you were ready to join in again. Your retreat would be covered by spearmen and archers; squires didn't get much of a look-in.

The real point to these tournaments was not to score points but to capture each other. Then, in order to win back his freedom, a prisoner had to pay a ransom. A strong jouster could make a good living at this game.

LEGEND 10: CIVIL WAR AND THE DEATH OF ARTHUR

THE BITTER END

With the disappearance of the Holy Grail, the kingdom of Logres began to fall apart. Sir Lancelot was abroad a lot trying to forget his love for Queen Guinevere. The other knights divided into goodies and baddies, and soon all the baddies were plotting against the Queen. First they tried to kill her, then they tried to get her condemned to death on a murder charge. Sir Lancelot came back to rescue her and forgot all about his good intentions – he was as much in love with her as ever. So then the baddies hatched a plot to catch him out. Here is the *Celtic Clarion* once again: the paper that brought you The Discovery of Arthur, bringing you his end with legend number 10:

Celtic Clarion

15 July

Was it Lance?
Massacre as unknown knight kills 13
Queen unharmed

Last night thirteen knights of the Round Table were killed – by one of their own brothers-in-arms!

The stairs of Carlisle Castle ran with blood. "There were bodies everywhere," said a castle servant. "We had to step over them to get to the Queen."

The incident occurred at 9.20pm when most of the servants had retired for the night. A band of fourteen fully-armed knights climbed the stairs to the Queen's apartment and broke down the door. In the fighting that followed, thirteen out of the fourteen intruders lay dead or badly injured – and Sir Lancelot was seen hurrying the Queen away from the scene.

Sir Gawain, the brother of one of the knights fatally injured in the fight, spoke to a reporter from the *Clarion*. He said his brother, Sir Agravaine, 34,

who has since died of his injuries, told Sir Gawain there was no doubt that the couple were together. "When they broke down the door, Agravaine said the Queen was in her shift – and Lance wasn't wearing much either," said Gawain.

LANCELOT CAUGHT WEARING NOT-A-LOT!

He said that Lancelot had dragged Sir Congrevaunce into the room, killed him and stolen his armour before emerging to fight the others.

"To kill your brother knights inside the King's palace is an outrage," said Sir Gawain. "Especially when those knights were defending the King's honour." He said that his brother, Agravaine, and the other knights had not died in vain. "At least the scandal is out in the open at last," he said. "The King cannot bury his head in the sand any longer. He will have to act."

TIME FOR ARTHUR TO FACE FACTS !!

Celtic Clarion

23 July

Queen to be burned at stake

Today King Arthur found his queen of 25 years guilty of adultery and ordered her to be burned at the stake.

At a meeting of the Knights of the Round Table, the Queen stood accused of adultery by Sir Gawain and Sir Mordred. No one spoke in her defence, and she showed no emotion when sentenced.

GUIN REMAINS COOL AS SHE HEARS "HOT" NEWS !!

The Queen lost her title at the same time. She no longer has the right to be called "Her Majesty" and will be executed at dawn tomorrow. The King also passed the sentence of death on Sir Lancelot if ever he dares show his face at court.

"It is all very sad," said a palace spokesman. "King Arthur turned a blind eye for many years for the sake of the kingdom. Now he has been forced to act. It must be a terrible moment for him – he is losing his wife and his best friend."

Celtic Clarion

24 July

Lance grabs Queen
24 dead in dawn raid

In a dramatic dawn raid which left 24 dead, loyal Lance du Lac descended on the procession leading Queen Guinevere to the stake and snatched her from the jaws of death.

Once again Lance has proved that there's not another fighter in the kingdom to touch him – and that while he is alive, no one will lay a finger on the Queen.

GUIN FINDS REFUGE IN THE ARMS OF LOVE!

Men had been up all night building the tall pyre to which the Queen was to be tied. The day dawned grey and cloudy, as if it had caught the mood of her subjects, most of whom were sad at the prospect of seeing her die a traitor's death.

A sad and weary King Arthur watched from the battlements as Guinevere was led out from the castle, dressed only in the smock of a common criminal. Below, Sir Gawain, Sir Mordred, Sir Gareth and Sir Gaheris, along with many other members of the Orkney family, angry at the deaths of their brothers, had formed the guard which led the Queen out to the stake.

But then before the procession was half-way across the courtyard a posse of fully armed knights fell on the procession.

Through the dust and flashing weapons it was possible to see the leopards on the shield of the leading knight. It was loyal Lance himself. Within minutes the Queen's jailors had fled, and the courtyard was full of injured knights and the sound of screaming.

IT'S LANCE TO THE RESCUE!!

The Queen stood pale and trembling until Sir Lance swept her up beside him on his horse. Then as quickly as they had arrived, the attackers galloped out of the castle.

Once again, the Queen's Knight has saved the Queen, this time from the King himself. But the price is high – another 24 knights killed – among them another of Sir Gawain's brothers, this time Sir Gaheris.

The *Clarion* shudders to think what this means for the Kingdom. Is Logres now about to descend into civil war? Does it make any sense now to speak of Logres, when everything it stood for is in ruins?

Celtic Clarion

8 August

War Edition
Battle for Joyous Garde
Loyal Lance spares King's life

A fierce battle was fought today at Sir Lance's seaside fortress, Joyous Garde, as the King and his troops hit back at Lancelot. Sir Lancelot has been sheltering the Queen there for the past six weeks.

Suddenly, in the midst of the carnage, the King and lusty Lance found themselves face to face.

"FANCY MEETING YOU HERE !!!"

The King hurled himself at Lancelot, but the Queen's Knight refused to strike back. Sir Bors rushed to his aid, and struck the King a blow with his lance, causing the King to fall from his saddle.

As he drew his sword, Sir Bors was heard to ask Lance, "Do you want me to end this war?" Loyal Lance cried, "No way! If you lay a finger on him I'll have your head." Then he dismounted and helped the King to his feet.

BIG-HEARTED LANCE LENDS A HELPING HAND!

The King turned away from his old friend with tears in his eyes.

The day ended with no clear victory for either side but the battle will continue tomorrow.

Celtic Clarion

15 August

Take back your Queen
Pope orders Arthur to forgive
"It's Lance or Me!" says Sir Gawain

The siege of Joyous Garde ended today when the King got a warning from the Pope. His Holiness is known to be very angry at the civil war in Britain. He told Arthur "Take back your Queen, or leave the Church".

Sources close to the King say that he is secretly delighted to have an excuse to end the war without loss of face. However, Sir Gawain, who has lost most of his family in the conflict, is furious. "The King will have to do as the Pope says," he told a reporter. "But if he lets lying Lance back as well I will have to seriously rethink my vow of loyalty."

Celtic Clarion

31 August

Lavish Lance returns Queen

GORGEOUS GUIN PLUMPS FOR A GOLDEN GOWN FOR A JOURNEY HOME TINGED WITH SADNESS!

Twenty-five years ago, a young and gallant knight called Sir Lancelot delivered a beautiful young bride-to-be to his friend and liege lord, Arthur. Today, a sad and weary man set out from Joyous Garde to deliver a frightened wife to her failing husband. It was not the stuff of fairy-tale romance – but Lavish Lance seemed determined to pretend. He had spent a fortune on the frocks.

187

For her return journey to Camelot, Guinevere wore a stunning dress of cloth of gold – and Lance wore a matching suit. A hundred knights, all dressed in green velvet, escorted them, each carrying an olive branch for peace. Twenty-four ladies-in-waiting, also in green velvet, attended the Queen, while Sir Lance had twelve young nobles in white riding behind him.

But the olive branches cut no ice when lover-boy Lance arrived at Camelot. The seats of the Round Table were all full of Lance's enemies. Gawain sat in Lance's old place at the King's right hand.

"WHO'S THAT SITTING IN MY CHAIR?!"

No sooner had Lance entered the court than Gawain accused him of murdering his brothers. Lance offered to walk barefoot from Carlisle to Sandwich in penance, but Gawain ordered him out of the country in fifteen days – and said he would follow him to the ends of the Earth to avenge his brothers.

"GET GONE!" GROWLS GRUMPY GAWAIN!

The King sat silent throughout. "He is not the man he was," said a squire, who refused to be named. "It's as if he's given up and is leaving everything to Gawain."

Sir Lancelot had left the court by nightfall – but not before promising the Queen that if she needed his help he would come to her. It is thought he will abandon Joyous Garde and live at his estates at Benwick in France.

6 months later...

Celtic Clarion

1 March

King hounds Sir Lance
Mordred left as Regent

Months of rumour ended today when the King and Sir Gawain set out at the head of a large army to lay siege to Sir Lancelot's estates in France.

Getting his Queen back has not soothed King Arthur's bruised ego. Reports say that the royal couple have not been getting on well. Now the King has left both Queen and Kingdom in the care of Sir Mordred, the youngest of his nephews.

WOULD YOU TRUST THIS MAN WITH YOUR WIFE?

The King's army is expected to reach France late this evening.

Intelligence sources there say that the King will not receive the chivalrous treatment he received at the siege of Joyous Garde.

"Lancelot's pals take the line that here he is an invader, and so has forfeited the right to be treated as their liege lord. It looks as if it could get pretty nasty," said an informant.

Celtic Clarion

25 May

Mordred is King
"Arthur and Lancelot dead in battle"

In a surprise statement last night, Sir Mordred announced that King Arthur and Sir Lancelot had died in single combat in France. He said he was now King of Britain and would shortly marry Queen Guinevere.

But sources in France deny the deaths.

The Queen who fled to the Tower of London at the news said she does not believe the reports. She also said she has no intention of marrying Sir Mordred.

"ME, MARRY MORDRED? YOU MUST BE MAD !!!"

Celtic Clarion

2 June

King Arthur lives!
from our special correspondent

Mordred was lying when he said King Arthur and Sir Lancelot are dead. Both men are alive and said to be in good health. But Arthur is raging at Mordred's treachery – and is on his way back to Camelot to give him a good hiding!

As soon as news reached King Arthur of Mordred's capers he ordered the siege of Benwick to be lifted.

"I'LL MURDER MORDRED" VOWS ARTHUR!

Arthur is marching home with his army to fight for his kingdom.

It won't be much fun for Mordred when he gets here!

Celtic Clarion

23 June

Battle of Dover Beach
Gawain badly injured

King Arthur succeeded in driving the traitor Mordred's troops from the Dover beaches today – but saw hundreds of his best knights killed and injured in the process.

191

Mordred had commandeered many small boats and sent his men out to attack the King's loyal knights as they tried to land. But King Arthur was not deterred and the plan backfired as he and his men hacked and slashed their way ashore. Many did not make it as, weighed down by heavy armour, they fell in the sea and drowned.

Those who did stagger on to the beach were attacked again. But Mordred's traitors were no match for the King's loyal knights. As night fell, Mordred saw victory slipping from him, and fled.

Tonight there are unconfirmed reports that Sir Gawain was badly injured in the battle.

"HEAVY METAL" CAUSES TROOP'S DOWNFALL!!

Celtic Clarion

24 June

Sir Gawain dies
Deathbed plea to Lancelot

Today, Sir Gawain of Orkney, nephew of King Arthur and heir to the throne, died of the wounds he sustained in yesterday's battle of Dover Beach.

But in a dramatic deathbed confession, he blamed himself for the country's chaos. "It is all because of my stupidity and pride that you knights had to fight here today," he said. "It's my fault that Lancelot was exiled. It was my need for revenge that meant the King left Mordred in charge."

Weak from his wounds, Sir Gawain asked for parchment and dictated a letter to Sir Lancelot.

"Come home and serve your King," he wrote.

Within minutes of signing the letter, Sir Gawain drew his last breath. He will be buried in the grounds of Dover Castle with full military honours.

GAWAIN CHOOSES "HUMBLE PIE" FOR FINAL FEAST!

Celtic Clarion

8 July

Carnage
Peace accord fails
Mordred dead, Arthur missing

King Arthur's attempt to bring peace to the kingdom was brought to an abrupt end today – by an adder!

193

In an attempt to save the kingdom from more suffering and slaughter, King Arthur last week offered to sign a peace treaty with his dangerous nephew Mordred. All week negotiators worked behind the scenes to try and agree the terms.

This morning it seemed they had succeeded. Both leaders, each accompanied by fourteen knights, met on a down at Camlann. Not far off their armies waited and watched. The atmosphere was tense but hopeful as the King and his nephew signed their names – but then disaster struck.

An adder slithered from the bracken, a young knight drew his sword to kill it, the other camp saw the flashing steel – and thought it signalled the call to arms. They blew their horns and drew their swords.

In the vicious fighting that followed, thousands of men lost their lives, including Sir Mordred.

Meanwhile, the King himself is missing. He was last seen towards the end of the battle lying injured in the arms of Sir Bedivere, but when the battle ended there was no sign of either man.

KNIGHT SLAYS SNAKE.
...... BIG MISTAKE!

Celtic Clarion

10 July

Secret burial at hermitage
Was it Arthur's body?

Rumours were rife yesterday about a mystery corpse which may have been the body of King Arthur. A number of strange ladies arrived at midnight at a hermitage near Camlann and asked the hermit to bury a man's body and pray for his soul.

MYSTERIOUS MAIDENS ON MIDNIGHT MISSION!

The hermit said the body was that of a tall, well-built man of about 50, who had died from battle wounds. He did not recognize any of the ladies, who were hooded, but said that they were obviously well-born. When asked if he thought the body was that of the King, the hermit said he could not be certain, but that it seemed likely.

If it was the King, who were the mystery ladies? They were not seen on the battlefield, so how did they get hold of the body? And why were none of King Arthur's knights in attendance?

If you saw this procession, or know anything about it, please call the *Clarion* Hotline on Logres 2468.

Celtic Clarion

12 July

'My King is dead'
Sir Bedivere speaks
EXCLUSIVE

Today, an exhausted Sir Bedivere walked in from the woods and told the *Clarion* of the last hours of Arthur, King of Britain.

MORDRED IS DEAD...YESSS!!

Sir Bed was with Arthur on the battlefield, and saw him kill Sir Mordred – but before he died, the wicked Mordred had dealt Arthur a mortal blow. "Sir Lucan and I went to help the King," said Bedivere. "We carried him off the battlefield, to a chapel nearby. But Sir Lucan was also badly injured. He died – and then it was just the King and me."

Sir Bedivere said the King knew he was near death. "He was full of sorrow about the fall of Logres, and he was bothered about his sword, Excalibur," he said. "He said Excalibur had come from the Lady of the Lake and that it should go back to her."

Sir Bedivere confessed that he had not wanted to obey the King's order and throw the sword into the lake. He felt it should be kept for the good of the kingdom.

So twice he hid it and returned to the King, telling him he had obeyed his orders. But the King did not believe him and called him a liar and a traitor. Weak though he was, Arthur threatened to kill him, and sent Sir Bed back to the lake again. This time Bed threw the sword as far as he could out into the water.

Then something happened which made the hair rise on his neck. "A woman's arm, clothed in silk rose from the water and caught the sword," he said. "It shook the sword three times at the sky before pulling it down into the dark water."

HOWZAT!!!

Bedivere went back to the King and told him what had happened. The King, weaker than ever, seemed pleased. He told Sir Bedivere he was dying and asked him to help him down to the water's edge.

"When we got there," said Bed, "a black barge had appeared from nowhere. It waited by the shore, hung with a black canopy, and full of ladies, all dressed in black. Among them were three queens, all with black veils over their faces, and crowns set upon their veils.

As I staggered down the beach with my King in my arms a great wail of sorrow went up from these ladies."

Very weak now, King Arthur asked Sir Bedivere to lay him in the barge.

Bed did as he was told – and as he laid the King's head in the lap of the first queen, he saw to his amazement that it was none other than his arch enemy, Morgan le Fay.

"She spoke to him," said Bed, "and her voice was gentle." She said, "Dear brother, why have you stayed away from me so long?"

ARTHUR AND BED SEE BARGEFUL OF BEAUTIES!

With that, Sir Bedivere stepped ashore as the barge moved silently away. It was then the shock hit him – the thousands dead, the end of the Round Table, the end of an era.

"I called out to my King, how can I go on alone?" said Sir Bedivere. "He called back – do the best you can. I must go to Avalon to be healed of my wound."

At that, Sir Bedivere said, he took heart, thinking this meant that King Arthur would be coming back. But then, as the barge slid silently out of sight, he heard him call again, his voice weaker than ever.

"If you never hear from me again, pray for my soul."

It was then Sir Bedivere knew he had seen his King and liege lord for the last time. "The Old Bear met his end just as Merlin had said he would, on the battlefield of Camlann," he told the *Clarion*.

THE FINAL FAREWELL!

When told of the ladies who delivered the body of a man to a local hermitage, Sir Bedivere agreed that they answered the description of the ladies in the barge into whose care he had delivered the dying king.

So King Arthur, King of Britain and the realm

of Logres, is no more. A great man is dead, and his country will miss him sorely. Though some have questioned the wisdom of some of his decisions in recent years, there is no doubt he did more to unify his country than any other king before him. He drove out the Saxons and created the world-famous order of the Knights of the Round Table, bringing standards of courage and honour, decency and order to Britain that had not been seen before. In the face of his wife's infidelity he maintained a dignified silence. He was unfailingly generous and chivalrous. We shall not see his like again. Truly, the days of King Arthur and the Knights of the Round Table will be remembered for ever.

With Mordred dead, King Arthur leaves no heir.

Did you know…?

In 1168 a messenger brought a letter from King Arthur to King Henry II of England? Henry was fighting rebels in Brittany (France) at the time. The letter told him to stop fighting "the subjects of King Arthur." Henry was not fazed by a letter from the Otherworld. He sent his reply back to Arthur with the same messenger. "Like Arthur, I am King of the whole island of Britain," he wrote. "If I win in Brittany, then the lands of the Britons both sides of the Channel will be reunited just like they were before the coming of the Saxon invaders." Then he had both letters – his and the one that supposedly came from Arthur – posted up so that everyone could see.

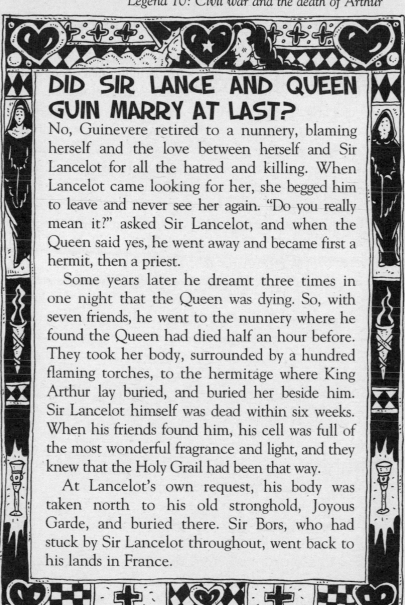

DID SIR LANCE AND QUEEN GUIN MARRY AT LAST?

No, Guinevere retired to a nunnery, blaming herself and the love between herself and Sir Lancelot for all the hatred and killing. When Lancelot came looking for her, she begged him to leave and never see her again. "Do you really mean it?" asked Sir Lancelot, and when the Queen said yes, he went away and became first a hermit, then a priest.

Some years later he dreamt three times in one night that the Queen was dying. So, with seven friends, he went to the nunnery where he found the Queen had died half an hour before. They took her body, surrounded by a hundred flaming torches, to the hermitage where King Arthur lay buried, and buried her beside him. Sir Lancelot himself was dead within six weeks. When his friends found him, his cell was full of the most wonderful fragrance and light, and they knew that the Holy Grail had been that way.

At Lancelot's own request, his body was taken north to his old stronghold, Joyous Garde, and buried there. Sir Bors, who had stuck by Sir Lancelot throughout, went back to his lands in France.

FANTASTIC FACTS 10: TEST YOUR KNOWLEDGE OF ARTHURIAN LEGEND ... AND WIN A TRIP FOR TWO TO THE MAGICAL OTHERWORLD BENEATH THE WATERS...

1 King Arthur was:
  a) found under a mulberry bush.
  b) washed up on the beach.
  c) born to Queen Igrayne after a night of passion with Uther Pendragon.

2 King Arthur found his sword Excalibur:
  a) sticking up out of a rock in the churchyard of Westminster Abbey.
  b) when he tripped over it on the palace steps.
  c) appearing from a lake attached to the arm of a mystery woman.

3 The best knight in the world was:
  a) Sir Gawain
  b) Sir Lancelot
  c) Sir Galahad

4 What animal(s) did Sir Lancelot have on his coat-of-arms?
  a) A unicorn
  b) Five parrots
  c) Three leopards

5 Sir Lancelot's girlfriend was:
  a) Queen Guinevere

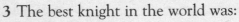
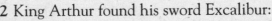

b) Elaine of Astolat
  c) Elaine of Carbonek

6 Which is a character in Arthurian legend?
  a) The Green Man
  b) The Green Giant
  c) The Green Knight

7 Morgan le Fay was married to:
  a) Merlin
  b) Sir Accolon
  c) King Uriens

8 Merlin disappeared because:
  a) he tried to walk on the lake, fell in, and drowned.
  b) Nimuë buried him under a rock.
  c) he went mad, killed his wife, and shut himself in a glass tower.

9 What happened to the Holy Grail after the knights Bors, Galahad and Percival had drunk from it?
  a) It vanished in a puff of smoke.
  b) They buried it and made a map marked hidden treasure.
  c) It went up to heaven on a sunbeam.

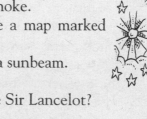

10) Why did Sir Gawain hate Sir Lancelot?
  a) He was jealous of him.

b) He felt sorry for King Arthur.

c) Sir Lancelot had killed two of his brothers.

Answers:

1 b) and **c)** are both legends about his birth. Bleys of Orkney, Merlin's teacher, told Queen Morgause that a naked baby had come riding to shore on a wave the night King Uther died; and the story more usually told is that Merlin cast a spell so that Queen Igrayne would think Uther was her husband Gorlois.

2 c) Excalibur appeared from a lake, held by a mystery woman. The sword in the churchyard did not have a name.

3 b) and **c)** Sir Lancelot was the best knight in the world for a long time, but then he blotted his copybook with the Queen; his son Galahad, who never tangled with ladies at all, then became the best knight in the world.

4 c) Three leopards were on Lancelot's shield.

5 a) and **c)** Lancelot was the Queen's Knight, which meant he was in love with her but didn't do anything naughty, at least for a while. Elaine of Astolat was in love with him, and he wore her favour to the tournament, but he was just doing her a good turn, he wasn't in love with her. Elaine of Carbonek was the mother of his child, Galahad. He would never have done it if she hadn't cast a spell on him, though at least that was his story.

6 c) The Green Knight is the character in the legend

who could pick up his head after it had been cut off. However, all three probably spring from the same fertility figure of Celtic legend.

7 c) Morgan le Fay tried to murder her husband Sir Uriens so she could marry Sir Accolon, but she didn't succeed.

8 b) and **c)** are both legends about the disappearance of Merlin.

9 c) The Holy Grail went up to heaven on a sunbeam.

10 c) Sir Agravaine was killed at Carlisle Castle when he tried to burst in on Sir Lancelot and the Queen. Sir Gaheris was killed when Sir Lancelot jumped on the procession leading the Queen to be burnt at the stake.

EPILOGUE

Who knows when the first stories about Arthur were told? Some people think from his own lifetime, some time in the fifth century AD, around campfires and in the halls of British chieftains. As the stories were passed down the ages, they grew and changed. Bits of one story got mixed up with another.

Not until 1136 does the Arthur we know and love today appear. Geoffrey de Monmouth wrote two books: *A History of the Kings of Britain* and *The Life of Merlin*, and Arthur shows up in both. These were supposed to be history but many people think he made it all up. Soon storytellers the length and breadth of Europe were retelling Geoffrey's 'history'. Among the most famous were the French troubadour, Chretien de Troyes, and Wolfram von Eschenbach, a German knight. People say that Wofram's story *Parzival* contains – in code – all the secrets of the Knights Templar, a group of real knights who were mysteriously rich and powerful in the twelfth century.

The tale we in Britain know best is *Morte d'Arthur* (Death of Arthur) written in the fifteenth century by Sir Thomas Malory while he was in prison for rebellion. Malory was a mate of Thomas Caxton, who invented the first printing press so the *Morte d'Arthur* was one of the first books ever to be printed (rather than copied by hand).

After that people lost interest in King Arthur for another few hundred years. Then in the nineteenth century, poets and musical composers got interested again. Since then works on Arthur have been pretty non-stop. There have been novels, plays, films, operas and TV scripts about Arthur and the Knights of the Round Table – not to mention a lot of books trying to explain the legends.

It's not surprising. They're great stories, full of mystery, romance and excitement. Why not tell them to your mates?